W9-DCM-397

Caught Between the Devil
and the Deep Blue Sea...

Jessie ripped off her boots and launched into a low dive from the bow, trying not to flinch in the face of the bullets angling down from the bank. She kicked out hard as the water closed over her head, swimming desperately, hoping to cover as much distance as possible before surfacing for breath. She heard the slap of lead hitting the choppy water, and wished she could have headed for the south shore instead—but the south was the side on which the churning, tearing jumble of boulders and falls began wedging out across the river, leaving her no choice but to go right toward Emil Pritt's gunfire.

━━◆ **WESLEY ELLIS** ◆━━

LONE STAR

AND THE
TIMBERLAND TERROR

J®

A JOVE BOOK

LONE STAR AND THE TIMBERLAND TERROR

A Jove Book/published by arrangement with
the author

PRINTING HISTORY
Jove edition/March 1986

All rights reserved.
Copyright © 1986 by Jove Publications, Inc.
This book may not be reproduced in whole
or in part, by mimeograph or any other means,
without permission. For information address:
The Berkley Publishing Group,
200 Madison Avenue, New York, N.Y. 10016.

ISBN: 0-515-08496-4

Jove books are published by The Berkley Publishing Group,
200 Madison Avenue, New York, N.Y. 10016.
The words "A JOVE BOOK" and the "J" with sunburst
are trademarks belonging to Jove Publications, Inc.

PRINTED IN THE UNITED STATES OF AMERICA

Chapter 1

When stealth means survival, man can outdo a coyote.

Outwardly the pair appeared to be slumped, weary travelers, unaware of their surroundings, and uncaring. And in keeping with this guise, as well as for comfort, both Jessie Starbuck and Ki wore well-worn jeans, dusty cotton shirts, and sweat-stained hats. Jessie did not appear to be what she really was—a proud, aristocratic woman in her mid-twenties; a crack shot with her now holstered revolver or the twin-shot derringer concealed behind her belt buckle; and a shrewd, knowledgeable heiress to immense wealth, the Starbuck international business empire. Nor did her companion and protector, Ki, seem to be more than a tall, lean man in his early thirties, of mixed Japanese and Caucasian blood, and so peaceful by nature that he lacked a gunbelt or any other sign of a firearm. In fact, though, he was a samurai-trained master of martial arts, in whose old leather vest were secreted short daggers and similar small throwing weapons, including razor-edged, star-shaped steel disks called *shuriken*.

In truth, they rode warily, merging their bodies with their mounts in what Ki would call the art of acting innocuous. Remaining carefully alert was difficult, for

1

rarely had they followed a more monotonous trail. There'd been no sounds other than muffled swishing through forest groves or hooves clopping over rock and gravel.

All yesterday they'd headed up the Sacramento Valley and during the night had followed the one and only wagon road high into the Siskiyou Mountains. At dawn they'd breached the summit. Since then the road had continued northerly through the Siskiyou Gap, gradually descending toward the timbered foothills and lush, rolling country of Oregon's Rogue River Valley. Occasionally from higher elevations they could see far ahead and were not surprised by the lack of movement or dust clouds. Emil Pritt had a good head start on them and was too experienced to leave any telltale signs of passage. But they had a basic notion where the man was heading—north, since east and west were hemmed by rugged, uninhabited mountain ranges—and they figured that sooner or later the man would have to stop in one of the small, scarce towns to rest, to replenish his supplies, or to deliver the stolen money. And then they'd nab him.

On the Oregon side of the Siskiyous, they reached the logmill community of Medford just after high noon. In short order they learned that Emil Pritt hadn't even paused here, so they kept on in dogged pursuit. Sun burned their eyes and the heat made sweat trickle into them and sting. Jessie removed her denim jacket. Ki licked his lips, tasting the salt of his perspiration. Both took their time, gauging the green, wooded terrain and wondering if Pritt suspected he was being trailed and had doubled around to wait in ambush.

The going became easier. Suddenly it struck Ki as strange that he saw no more signs of animal life. The jays that had been squawking in low branches were silent now, and not even a gray squirrel darted across open fields. Motioning to Jessie, he pulled up in short, black shadows of trees and sat stiff and listening in the saddle. Then his roan whinnied and they heard an answer from around the blind curve just ahead.

Cautiously they approached, hands hovering near weapons. Jessie was about to suggest they leave the road and skirt around through the trees, when they heard a man's gravelly voice declare, "Okay, Rachel, that oughta do it."

If Rachel gave a response, it was too low to catch. Instead came a creak of springs, the snap of a whip, and the trundling grumble of iron wheels. By then Jessie and Ki were at the bend, where they saw a large, battered freight wagon. The words INDIANA TO THE CASCADES OR BUST had been smeared on its patched canvas hood with a brush and identified the couple riding the box seat as Hoosiers.

Trotting alongside, Jessie and Ki eyed the couple. The driver was a husky, tanned man in his mid to late thirties, clad in linsey-woolsey shirt and butternut pants and wearing a cartridge bandolier across his muscular chest. Beside him sat an auburn-haired girl of no more than twenty and probably less, her nubile body covered by a blue brocade dress.

Ki called out, "Having trouble? Can we help?"

"No sir, friend, but thanks." The driver wasn't handsome, but he had a likeable smile. "Had to pry a rock outta one horse's forehoof, is all," he added.

"Has anyone passed you recently?" Jessie asked.

"Yep. A man headin' our way, less'n an hour ago."

"Short? Heavyset?"

"Well, he was built more sideways than up'n down.

3

Was blond and bearded, and a gold tooth showed when he opened his mouth."

"And he swore at us," the girl interjected indignantly.

Jessie glanced at Ki. "Pritt. We're catching up."

After an exchange of friendly nods, they passed the wagon and soon left it out of sight behind them. The road flanked a steep ravine for about the next three miles; then it wandered in long curves following hill contours. Long before now the land along this stretch had been cut over, and in another ten years the pulp buyers would be bidding for the second-growth timber that was covering it. Soon the road dipped to the southern bank of the Rogue River, went along the edge for a bit, and finally ended at a clearing by a ferry dock.

Swift and treacherous, the Rogue was notorious for breaking unexpectedly into riffles or plunging into boat-crushing rapids. It offered superb fishing, but most of the year it could be used only to float logs of pulping size. The spring melt could be depended upon to give at least a week of high water and carry a logger's winter cut downstream to mill towns and ports.

The Rogue earned its name. Not surprisingly, therefore, this ferry was the only one plying the dangerous waters for a stretch of better than fifty miles. The landing slip on the north bank was a connection with the famous McKenzie Trail, which followed the Willamette Valley northward beyond Oregon and into the territory of Washington and beyond that into the Canadian wilderness. The ferry scow was docked at the far landing slip when Jessie and Ki rode into the clearing.

Through a ship's brass spyglass, the ferry tender spotted their waving hail. He cased the spyglass and levered the engine into gear, tossing a chunk of wood into the fire for good measure. Big pulleys whined on posts above the landing, as twin cables guided the bargelike craft slowly, agonizingly slowly, across the turbulent river, and Jessie and Ki chafed impatiently.

"Now Pritt's gaining a lead," Jessie murmured testily.

"He has to draw in somewhere," Ki reminded her. "He can't be any less tired and hungry than we are, and he hasn't changed horses since Redding. I wouldn't doubt he'll fold for the night when he hits Grants Pass, the next town up the line." Ki paused thoughtfully, swabbing his bronzed cheeks with a bandanna neckerchief. "Or do you suppose Pritt's taking the cutoff to Sweetgum instead?"

Jessie hipped around in the saddle and gazed in a general northeasterly direction, where a few miles from the main road lay the remote logging settlement of Sweetgum. She shook her head. "We've got our troubles at Sweetgum, what with the restraining order against Emerald Timber and all, but I don't think it's connected with Pritt."

"Probably not. Do you want to visit Sweetgum anyway?"

"On our return, perhaps, after we've dealt with Pritt. Then will be time enough." Jessie spoke tersely, a reflection of the bitter thoughts that were roiling through her as she considered the problems that were crowding in on them.

As was all too often the case, the immediate, major problem involved the cartel. The cartel was her implacable enemy, just as it had been her father's enemy dating from when he'd been a struggling young entrepreneur in the Orient. He'd run afoul of its ruthless henchmen early on and had fought its drug trade and slave trafficking with all his resources. The cartel's response was to murder Alex Starbuck's wife, Jessie's mother, while Jessie was still a babe.

Alex Starbuck responded in kind, and thus began the protracted warfare between him and the cartel. The deeper Alex delved into the machinations of his enemy, the more it became clear that the cartel's main goal was nothing less than the domination of the commercial and political interests of the young, growing United States. Eventually, one of the cartel's insidious tentacles managed to assassinate Alex Starbuck. But by then, Jessie was old enough and had the strength and cunning to take his place. After avenging her father's death, she pledged to use her inherited Starbuck fortune and influence to continue his battle until the entire cartel was utterly destroyed.

Helping Jessie was Ki, born in Japan to an American and his Japanese wife. From his father, Ki had inherited his respectable height and sinewy endurance; from his mother he'd been blessed with his lustrous black hair and almond-shaped eyes; from both had come his handsome bronze complexion. Orphaned at an early age, Ki had learned how to survive in a hostile world as a half-breed outcast and had eventually apprenticed himself to one of Japan's last great samurai, the aged Hirata. After Hirata's death, Ki had migrated to San Francisco, where he'd been hired by Alex Starbuck. When, years later, Alex was killed, Ki became the confidante and protector of Jessie to whom he was like an older brother. And, like Jessie, Ki hated the cartel with a passion.

Now, less than a week ago, the cartel had struck again. A Starbuck courier had been slain while leaving Sacramento aboard the Central Pacific, and his tote of negotiable bearer bonds swiped and hastily converted to cash— $256,733.28, to be exact, as Jessie subsequently learned from the fence who'd handled the transaction. By coincidence Jessie and Ki were in San Francisco at that

6

time. But explaining how they arrived at the scene of the crime so swiftly was not easy, nor was it easy to explain why they decided to take a direct hand in retrieving the money. They had discovered the cartel was behind the robbery, so they acted swiftly.

There was no question that the cartel was involved. The captured fence identified Emil Pritt as the man who'd sold him the bonds, and Emil Pritt had quite a lengthy entry in Jessie's small black notebook of cartel members. Her book was a copy of the original notebook, which was kept under lock and key back at her Circle Star Ranch in Texas. The original was old and worn, dating from when her father began listing every person and business connected with the criminal syndicate. Since his murder, Jessie had continued to update its entries. In it, she found that Pritt was a thug and a bandit, a cagey, utterly unscrupulous cartel strong-arm.

Immediately Jessie and Ki began to search for him. Their checking was sufficiently informal not to raise suspicions, but acute enough to follow gossip as weak and elusive as fireflies. They quickly picked up Pritt's getaway trail at Redding, up near the California base of the Siskiyous. In a sense they'd been lucky. They'd no way of knowing that Pritt's mount would contract spavin from overexertion, or that they'd arrive so soon after Pritt had traded horses. And it'd been luck that the single liveryman was a skinflint codger loving to haggle and boast of his bargaining with "a whiskery tub leading a winded, lame pinto," as he referred to Pritt.

The liveryman had been lucky as well, not to have had his head blown off. Pritt had no patience or respect for human life other than his own, and he must've had good reason to swallow his temper, or for that matter, not to have simply stolen a fresh mount. Jessie suspected it was because Pritt wanted to avoid so much as a whiff of alarm, and the only reason for that had to be because the cartel was brewing a real dose of trouble, financed by the money from the stolen bonds. There had been a sort of honorable lull before the lead-slinging storm of . . . Well, of what she did not know, but she sorely wished to learn.

So a stranger resembling Pritt had headed over the mountains on a bay. Jessie and Ki had pursued him to this ferry and were momentarily stymied on the wrong side of the Rogue—but in the right locale for the secondary problem involving Sweetgum and the surrounding timberland leased to the Starbuck-owned Emerald Timber Company. It was troublesome and threatening to become nastier, yet Jessie couldn't see a link between it and the cartel, much less Pritt.

Moreover, this secondary problem had been dragging on for some time now. Late last year, a Starbuck timber cruiser named Eliot Gideon discovered that the Cascade Range foothills above Sweetgum held clear pine and fir of premium quality. Quickly a subsidiary company, Emerald Timber, was created; Eliot was promoted to manager and, with his wife Margot, put in charge of Emerald; and sixty sections were leased from the financially ailing Oregon & California Railroad.

In the spring the Gideons moved in their crew and equipment and started logging. Also, in order to build up a head of water so logs could be floated down to the sawmill and railhead at Grants Pass, a dam was begun across a Rogue River tributary that flowed through the property. Scarcely were things in full swing, when Emerald was hit with a court order blocking further operations.

The injunction was brought by Liam McManus, owner of the Bar M, a cattle ranch below and adjacent to Emerald. McManus had just purchased his land from a beef syndicate and claimed in court that Emerald's logging would ruin the watershed for cattle grazing, while the dam would deprive his herds of their water supply. In turn, Starbuck lawyers found that the syndicate had no right to sell the land to McManus and were confident the courts would decide in favor of Emerald before it was all over. But if Emerald didn't log now during the summertime, it'd suffer irreversible losses by fall, when the heavy snows would keep the crew out of the woods— and it'd take that long to settle the case, not counting delays and appeals.

Eliot Gideon would not see the fall. The previous month, Gideon was brutally beaten and left for dead on the wagon trail to Sweetgum. He never regained consciousness, nor were his unknown assailants caught. His widow requested, and was granted, permission to stay on as sole manager, and so far she seemed to be working out, a thoroughly competent and well-respected woman by all accounts. Still, her Emerald crew was restive and blamed the Bar M cowpokes, and lumberjacks aren't known for keeping tea-party manners. Recently there'd been exchanges of insults and accusations, and there were a few fistfights and brawls in Sweetgum. It hadn't degenerated into knives or guns, not yet, but it could at any time.

Time. Time for the Emerald problem was running out, but that problem wasn't as immediate, as critical, as catching Pritt. And now, Jessie saw it was time to board the ferry.

"A buck a horse, four bits a human," the rheumy-eyed tender declared as he moored the scow. "Walk your horses on and hold 'em steady. No mountin' 'em while we're in motion."

While paying, Jessie asked, "Did you just take a man across?"

The tender nodded while he bit Jessie's coins to test their genuineness. Suddenly there came a whooping and clattering as the Hoosiers drove up in their wagon.

"Don't leave!" the girl cried. The man braked to a halt.

"Weren't goin' far or for long," the tender responded with a shrug. "Two bucks the team, a buck for you two, five for the wagon."

The man hesitated, glancing around. "We're supposed to meet my father here at the ferry. Zachary Biggs. D'you know him?"

"Ol' Zack, the trapper? Sure, everyone hereabouts knows Ol' Zack. Ain't seen him in a month o' Sundays, though. I heard tell there's a pelt buyer in Grants Pass now, so perhaps he's gone there."

The Indianans exchanged glances. The man fished a leather sack from under the wagon seat and from it drew some crumpled bills and a handful of small change, which he counted to the last penny. The tender accepted their money, gave them much the same instructions as he had Jessie and Ki, and then waited for them to drive aboard before casting off.

The tug of the current pulled the ferry from the south bank. Holding their horses, the four passengers stood fairly close to one another, and after a few moments, the man called out an amiable greeting to Jessie and Ki.

"Howdy! Looks like we bump again, don't it? M'name's Duncan Biggs, and this's my niece, Rachel. We're from Fort Wayne, Indiana."

Jessie introduced herself and Ki, and then remarked, "I gather you're planning to settle in this area."

"Yep. Aim to homestead and hunt, like my brother and pa do. Great country, Oregon, but sure's expensive." Duncan Biggs chuckled ruefully, jerking a thumb toward the ferry tender. "Took most all we got to get this far, but we'll have plenty of money soon's we hitch up with m'pa. Tain't like him to miss a meetin', though—"

"Uncle Dunc! You talk too much," his niece intervened tartly, a rosiness of embarrassment and annoyance showing on her face. She had, Ki saw as his eyes swept her with an appraising glance, features that were at once delicate and firm: mouth wide and stubborn, a nose angled at a delicate tilt. It was her eyes that caught and held him—eyes darker than her auburn hair, challenging him when she caught his notice of her. She continued to chastise her uncle, "You know Dad and Granddad always warned us not to chat with strangers. It's simply common sense."

Whatever Biggs was going to say in reply was cut off by a loud splash alongside the ferry. An instant later he was being pulled to the deck by Jessie, and his niece was being tossed by Ki, as one of the parallel cables collapsed over the ferry, its four-inch girth writhing like a giant serpent.

With a muttered oath, the tender grabbed an old rifle propped next to the steam engine and headed toward the prow of the ferry barge. Staring across the narrowing waters toward the north bank, he was in time to see, along with Jessie and Ki, a man chopping at the remaining cable that kept the ferry from drifting downstream. The man was half-hidden by waist-high brush, but enough of him showed to indicate that he was about five feet five and a good two hundred pounds big with a fat belly and arms like tree trunks. A gold tooth sparkled in his mirthlessly grinning mouth. "Emil Pritt!" Jessie gasped, even as his swinging double-bladed axe slashed. The cable snapped, ripping through the river's surging flow.

Swearing, the tender shouldered his rifle and triggered a shot at the man, only to see him duck out of sight in a nest of boulders. From the rocks came an answering blast, and the tender jerked around, a carbine bullet tunneling his chest. The ferry scow, caught in the angry surge of the Rogue's currents, was wheeling dizzily now. The tender, thrown off balance, flopped over the bow of the scow and vanished under the whirlpools.

Jessie tried to target Pritt with her swiftly drawn revolver, but the man was too well hidden and the ferry was wrenching too violently for effective aim. The horses were prancing and neighing, their eyes wide and white, and the wagon was beginning to wobble and sway hazardously. It was virtually all the four passengers could do just to hang on and avoid being stomped by the skittish horses. They were utterly powerless to stop the cut cables from running through the supporting pulleys and sinking from sight. And then, over the panicked trumpeting of their animals, they heard more sharp cracks of gunfire from the north bank. Slugs whipped past them, ricocheting off the chugging steam engine and splintering deep into the wood of the ferry and wagon.

"We're lost!" Biggs groaned. "We're gonna capsize f'sure—and if we don't drown, we'll be riddled with lead an' sink!"

His precocious niece hunched, transfixed with horror, and Jessie and Ki exchanged grim, alarmed glances. A deadly fate awaited them down the cliff- and forest-hemmed canyons of the Rogue: rapids, perhaps even waterfalls, and definitely a bushwhacker's bullets. The trapped quartet stood to lose their lives as well as their worldly possessions.

Chapter 2

Huddled and down on their knees in order to keep from being thrown from the deck of the pitching ferry, the four passengers saw the rush of the current sweep them closer to the south bank of the river, where fanglike rocks protruded above the water's surface. And though a sharp curve in the channel had put them out of sight of the ferry landing, the killer who'd cut them adrift was spurring his horse along the north bank and firing after them.

Ki was desperately trying to keep the horses from bolting. Duncan Biggs lunged for the dead tender's fallen rifle as another blast of lead ripped into the ferry. Only the cumbersome craft's wild bobbing and twisting kept Emil Pritt from picking them or the horses off in easy order—but it would also prevent Jessie from dispatching Pritt, should he close to within effective pistol range.

Another bullet pinged off the boiler of the pounding engine. The deflected slug seared across the rump of the nearest horse, which whinnied in shock and pain and lashed out kicking, catching Rachel a glancing blow on her spritely, round rump. Staggering, legs buckling, the girl careened against the low bulwark of the ferry, and with a keening cry, tumbled over the edge, striking open

15

water on the downriver side and plunging under the surface.

Without a breath of delay, Ki leaped for the rail and dived after her, ignoring the bullet that whined past his head. Dazed and gasping, Rachel surfaced, only to be caught by the surging current. Ki swam furiously in an effort to intercept her. He reached out, missed, stroked, and reached again, fingers tightening on the collar of her jacket. Then he battled for the bank, trying to resist the tide that was inexorably sweeping them toward boulders through which the river was cascading in deadly, foaming rapids.

Like Ki, Duncan Biggs had lunged after his niece. But he was on the other side of the horses and wagon and reached the bulwark too late to grab her. "Rachel!" he yelled, as he saw her and Ki rolling momentarily on the crest of a wave and then disappear. "Hang on, gal, hang on! I'm comin'!"

"No!" Again Jessie tackled Biggs, bringing him down before he could jump overboard. "They've gone too far for us to be able to help in time. Ki's a good swimmer, and he's the only one who's got a chance to save her." Sweat and spray riveted down Jessie's face, but in spite of the intense peril, she was calm and could think clearly. "Quick now—we've got our own saving to do!"

"But..." Distraught and confused, Biggs muttered and watched Jessie spring to her horse, then to Ki's, grabbing the coiled lariats from the pommels and hastily tying an end of one rope to the other.

"Do you think you can get to the bank with this?" Jessie asked, tossing him a portion of the line. "If you can snag it on one of the rocks before the sandbar coming up ahead, we'll miss being smashed in the rapids!"

"I–I, ah, can't swim," Biggs confessed.

"Great. And you were going to save your niece," Jessie muttered under her breath, fastening a loop around her waist with a slipknot. "Okay, hold the rope tight and cover me with that rifle."

Biggs snatched up the line and wound it firmly over a hardwood mooring bit. Simultaneously, Jessie ripped off her boots and launched into a low dive from the bow, trying not to flinch in the face of the bullets angling down from the bank. She kicked out hard as the water closed over her head, swimming desperately, hoping to cover as much distance as possible before surfacing for breath. She heard the slap of lead hitting the choppy water and wished she could have headed for the south shore instead—but the south was the side on which the churning, tearing jumble of boulders and falls began wedging out across the river, leaving her no choice but to go right toward Emil Pritt's gunfire.

When it seemed as though she would have to breathe and let the treacherous river water into her lungs, Jessie strove for the surface. She gasped for air and had a momentary glimpse of the ferry wallowing some yards behind and tangential to her. Duncan Biggs was shouting encouragement at her while firing the rifle as fast as he could load—with what, Jessie had no idea, but he must've located extra ammunition somewhere.

Jessie went under and struggled diagonally through the swift current. Emil Pritt sent a handful of bullets to pepper the spot where she'd been an instant before. Biggs' defending fire, however, had slowed Pritt's advance along the bank, and Jessie prayed that the killer would remain stymied. If he reached the sandbank before or during her arrival, she'd be in a worse fix than ever, a pointblank target as she climbed out of the water.

Once more she surfaced, got her bearings, and surged the short stretch to the bank as fast as she could. The last few feet she waded in the water until, exhausted and stumbling for balance, she freed the slip-knot and tied the rope around a granite boulder.

The lariat snapped taut, and for an instant it seemed impossible that it could hold the pull of the ferry. The current was strong and fought hard to hold its impetuous grip, yet now its force acted in their favor. Stalled in midriver and downstream of the boulder, the ferry yanked around in a dizzy arc, then reeled joltingly as its flat keel grounded on a brush-covered sandbar which had been thrust out into the river by a landslide in years past.

Grinning, sucking air into her lungs, Jessie lurched over and up on to the sandbar, eyes straining for sign of Emil Pritt.

"We're stuck solid!" Biggs panted, his voice trembling with relief as he jumped from the ferry on to dry land. "Now to find Rachel—"

They were found instead by Pritt. From the stony bluff above, his carbine repeater sent bullets stitching around Jessie and Biggs.

"Into the rocks!" Jessie shouted. "Get out of sight!"

They scrambled for cover as orange flashes and cracks of gunpowder burst from the brush-clumped, notched cliff. Slugs hit the ferry. Earthen grit and rock shards flew into Jessie's face. She hunkered with Biggs in the first, low-cropped fringe of boulders, pinned down. Her firearms were water-soaked, and their only other weapons were the aged rifle Biggs still clasped and a Bowie knife she glimpsed sheathed to his belt. She was gratified that so far she and Biggs had miraculously escaped harm,

18

but she knew that at any second one or both of them could expect to be hit.

She turned to Biggs. "Lend me your knife."

Courteously he obliged, though he asked, "What for?"

"What for! We've got to take that man out, that's what for."

"You?" Biggs was genuinely appalled. "You're mad."

"Mad enough to want to live—which neither of us will be soon at this rate. And it's up to me to try first," she stated, in a tone brooking no argument. "Believe me, I'm handy with a blade, and you seem to have gotten the hang of that miniature cannon." She avoided another pressing reason—wanting to retrieve the money without Biggs becoming the wiser. She added as she began crawling away, "Well, start shooting! Hold him down, keep him busy, and distract his attention, while I, ah, make a stab at it."

Grudgingly Biggs hefted the rifle and let fly a charge. When the cloud of black powder lifted, Jessie was gone.

During the frantic moments while Jessie and Biggs were struggling to salvage the ferry along with their lives, Ki had been helping Rachel fight out of the tugging current to head toward the bank. One hand still gripping her collar, he gestured with his other in front of her frightened face, pointing toward the sandbar. It was the best spot to head for, as Jessie was also about to determine, though, of course, Ki was unaware of this at the time.

He and Rachel thrashed toward the bar. They were scarcely past midriver, however, when a rotten branch off some long-gone tree reared out of the surface and rammed into Rachel. Ki's grasp was torn loose, and

Rachel was thrust, rolling, back into the hold of the swirling flow. Ki made a lunge for her, but she was already gone, plunging by the sandbar and into the whirling rapids.

Ki speared after her, swimming now with the current in a furious effort to intercept her. He came up alongside as she floundered, panting and choking, obviously in trouble.

"Grab on to me!" he called.

Immediately, unquestioningly, she obeyed. She clasped her arms around his neck from behind, and he moved ahead with a powerful stroke. Yet it was too late to avoid the rapids, and into the bone-smashing torrent they sailed, tumbling from boulder to boulder, desperately trying to elude puncturing flotsam and hammering maelstroms and white-spuming waterfalls.

It seemed like agonizing hours, but it only lasted minutes. Then they were spit out, groggy and gagging, into a churning pool at the base of the rapids. They came up for air. Treading water, they heard above the thunder of the rapids the sharp echoes of rifle fire from upriver. Ki resumed swimming toward the north bank, but progress was slow. Rachel was exhausted and mainly floating, confident that Ki would bring her to safety.

Finally his rope-soled slippers scraped against stone, and Ki dug in for better footing, half climbing, half crawling into a shallow break. The backwash of this break in the bank created a swirling eddy, and two or three strokes took them to the river's edge, where by clutching at an overhanging limb of a spruce, Ki was able at last to haul them both out of the cold, rushing water.

He half dragged her across to a patch of warm grass.

20

She was laughing deliriously, but did not appear to be hurt.

"You saved me!" she panted, and then she laughed again.

"But not your uncle or Jessie," Ki said, grimly listening to the sporadic exchange of gunfire. "C'mon, we've got to get back."

"No!" She grabbed his arm. "Sit down. Rest."

"No time for that!"

"Don't leave me alone! Please, just a second. I'm pooped." She pulled Ki down beside her, and it was then he noticed that her exertions had worked open the upper buttons of her dress, exposing her firm, perky breasts to view. "Anyway, Ki, I want to thank you."

"No thanks necessary," he replied gruffly, wondering whether he should mention the buttons or let her discover them for herself. He found her peek-a-boo dishabille much more intriguing than if she'd been stripped bare, the Oriental in him believing a woman naked is a woman shorn of her mystery. Rachel had a sort of vixenish appeal that put notions in his brain. He knew he should get on with getting back before those notions became physically evident.

So Ki moved. Then she moved and kissed him. "I'm not out of my mind, don't worry," she cooed, nibbling his ear. "I never could've made it myself, and this is how I want to thank you."

"Fine. Now you've thanked me."

"Not enough." And she kissed him again, harder.

She was young—not too young, but young enough— and time was pressing, but it was difficult to resist temptation. Ki kissed her in return, his lips laving down her neck. "No, no . . ." she mewed, wriggling without drawing away. Then he moved to her breasts, which had preoccupied him so tantalizingly. "Oh, that tickles," she gasped. "Stop." Ki stopped and stood up, chuckling. "I thought you said you wanted to thank me."

She regarded him and then lowered her eyes—partly in assumed modesty, partly to see the state of his readiness, which perhaps alarmed her. "I do . . . But I thought you wouldn't insist on it."

Rachel was a tease, Ki realized. That was all right by him. She'd taken a moment to pull her ploy, it was now out of her system, and they could start their return without further delay. "Up and at 'em, Rachel. I'm insisting. Your uncle and Jessie are under fire."

"You're right," she admitted, scrambling to her feet. "But I really was awfully winded. Oh, if anything's happened to Uncle Dunc . . ."

Ki took her by the hand and began propelling her quickly along the bank. "If something has, you won't be alone," he consoled. "You've still got your grandfather and father to be with."

"Father!" she exclaimed, in a deprecating tone. "Uncle Dunc's been more a father to me, even if he is—was—a gambler. Dad never got along much with Mom, and left with Granddad to seek his fortune here and then send for us. Or so he said. But we ain't heard a word from him for almost a year now. It was Granddad who persuaded us to pull stakes after Mom died, sell the farm, and come to Oregon with the notion of homesteading and trapping. Say, I still hurt where the horse kicked me. Can't you slow down?"

Ki shook his head and continued forging swiftly through the trees and brush that bordered the river, their pace helping the strong midday sun to dry their clothes. "There's plenty of land and pelts for the asking in these parts," he said. "But this is primitive country, and supplies and equipment can be mighty expensive. I hope you and your uncle came with enough money."

"You know darn well we didn't," she retorted breathlessly. "You saw Uncle Dunc scraping the bottom of the bag to pay the ferryman. Matter of fact, we left with a big poke, but he lost most of it in a card game in Kansas City—when he played a fifth ace. But Dad and Granddad have been trapping all last fall and winter, and Granddad wrote they'd clean up a fortune with the stash of pelts they'd made. We'll have lots of money soon's they sell them, if they haven't already."

Abruptly, as Rachel lapsed silent, Ki grew aware that the gunfire upriver had also ceased. The sudden quiet was ominous. Veering, he thrust through some entangling foliage and poised on the bank, craning for a clear view and fearing the worst.

Rachel squeezed in beside him, then pointed, smiling. "Look, the ferry's turning for that sandbar. They've got it controlled!"

Ki nodded. "It appears the rifleman's given up, too."

"Now we don't have to hurry so fast. They're safe!"

"But they'll be worried about us, and we—"

"The kick I got," she cut in groaning, soulfully wincing. "I've got such an ache there. I bet I've got a big bruise." She stepped back a pace, just enough to conceal her in the overhanging copse and give her room to gather her damp dress and lift it to her waist. She turned and pouted over her shoulder at Ki. "Do you see a bruise?"

Rachel was not wearing pantaloons, bloomers, a corset, or anything else under her dress. She was buck naked, her plump little bottom showing rosy and dappled in the filtered sunlight.

Ki became aroused, but he was also growing weary

23

of her flirting. He wondered how far he could get with her, or rather, how far she'd go before turning off again. In any case, the quickest cure seemed to be a dose like before, so he stepped close, slid an arm around her, and kissed her. She reacted with enthusiasm, the pressure of her body like an eager promise.

He began to fondle one of her breasts. She leaned away and smiled tauntingly up at him. "Are we going to start that again?"

"No, we're ending it," he replied, lowering his hands. "C'mon, drop your dress and your act, and let's be on our way."

"What's the matter?" She flared. Her mouth went down at the corners, while her eyes went soft, and she just stood there with her dress hiked, running her other hand across her lower belly and buttocks and then dipping it between her thighs. "I ache, Ki. I really ache badly," she mewed. "I ache all over."

So that was her game! Her denials were just for the record, in case anyone should accuse her of being too easy. Ki caught her by both shoulders and kissed her again. She glued her mouth to his, eyes closed, nostrils quivering, her curious fingers now moving to find the bulge at his groin and traveling its length. She made a whimpering sound in her throat, still not breaking the kiss, her hand sliding to his waist. Deftly she untied his rope belt and popped the top button. She lifted her mouth from his and twisted slightly, Ki sensing she was hot with anticipation as she unbuttoned his fly and tugged his jeans down. He arched his hips, and she used both hands to grasp and begin to massage the exposed shaft of his erection.

"You said we're in a hurry, so hurry," she whispered

throatily, "but not on the ground. The ground's hard; it'll hurt my back."

"Not going to take this lying down, eh?" Ki positioned his crotch against her, while she wriggled in an odd mixture of trepidation and desire, gingerly reaching between her legs to aim him toward her pink cleft. Flesh met flesh, seeking that rapturous lodging, the hard within the soft. As the experienced martial artist conquered by seeming to yield, so the female conquered by accepting the thrust.

"God, you feel so good," she sighed, as he slid, rigid and thick, deep inside her. She was small, tight. He felt compressed by moist softness, surrounded by slick heat. He began to pump.

"This is insane," she panted, pistoning against him. "But I tell you, Ki, I tell you true, if I don't get my itch scratched once a week, I simply fall to pieces. And the week's up."

Ki paused. "You mean you schedule this?"

"Sexing should never be haphazard. That'd be like animals."

Ki started thrusting again, unwilling to argue. Rachel moaned deliriously, half standing and half crouching as she ground against him, hoping to impale herself.

It was a harsh, quick union. Ki hammered into her greedy depths, while she gasped and humped in concert—wanton, lost in lust, with her devouring frenzy stimulating Ki to a savage tempo. She undulated her thighs in a mania of passion, heaving her womanhood back against him and then, to make it more fulfilling, reaching a hand to massage his scrotum gently.

Her rhythm increased as her orgasm approached. It was Ki, however, who climaxed first. He released so fast, so furiously, that he was almost chagrined—until he realized that she, too, was pounding and squeezing inner muscles in time with his pulsing. Soft muscles moved in spasms of delight, enclosing him tightly, throbbing ecstatically. She bent her legs wider, pushing back with pelvic force, trapping the final sparks of pleasure.

"You like?" She giggled a happy, rippling sound of joy.

"I like," Ki sighed, withdrawing.

Rachel straightened, letting her dress fall and primly smoothing out its wrinkles with her hand. "There's more next week—"

Her invitation was shattered by the sudden, savage bark of rifle fire. Ki, hitching up his jeans, sprang to the bank.

"They're in trouble again!" he snapped. "It looks like they're pinned down on the sandbar. C'mon, Rachel, let's go!"

She needed no urging. She raced after Ki as he sped upriver through the dense growth.

Chapter 3

By now Jessie had wormed through the sandbar's weedy scrub and boulders to the base of the riverbank, where she crouched motionless for a moment as she considered her next move.

Thicker underbrush covered the slope to the crest of the bank, and from there on stretched a rising jumble of stony outcrops and pine forests. And Emil Pritt. He was up there in the rocks with his loot and carbine, commanding the sandbar and planning to leave no witnesses to his escape. Against Pritt, Jessie had only Biggs' hunting knife, yet she was determined to stop him from slaying and fleeing. She hoped she could capture him alive to answer her questions, but if it came down to kill or be killed, so be it.

First, though, she had to get to him.

Hunching low, Jessie worked her way up the sloping bank in a circuitous route, wishing to hurry yet knowing her only prayer lay in avoiding detection. She didn't hesitate at the top of the bank, but plunged on through shifting sunlight and shadows, the resinous scent of the pines heavy about her. Her bootless footfalls were muffled by Pritt's carbine and Biggs' rifle. Suddenly the

27

fringe of trees dropped away to a narrow field that ended at a lift of broken wall.

Again she chose a roundabout course, darting across the field in a wide, concealing curve that left her better positioned to climb above and behind Pritt without being spotted. Starting upward and needing both hands free, she clenched the knife between her teeth, while she cautiously navigated the steep hillside. Occasionally she paused to shade her eyes and study carefully the lay of the rise, trying to ascend through the screening growths and raw crevices in a looping hairpin swing that would bring her to where she could get the drop on Pritt. Easier said than done! When he'd holed up in the rocks, Pritt had picked his spot with deadly skill.

Rifle shots continued to be traded, a haze of smoke wafting from a ledge to her left and marking Pritt's vantage point amid a crop of staggered rock slabs that cut off her view of him. But that meant he probably couldn't see her. She did catch a glimpse of Pritt's horse, its saddlebags bulging, as she climbed higher at an angle in order to approach the ledge from above, on the killer's blind side.

She was almost to that spot when both men ceased firing, perhaps to reload, perhaps because they were hit. Jessie flattened, forcing herself to advance slowly and very gently across a short embankment of loose shale and gravel. She was close, not more than twenty yards, yet the footing was treacherous. Despite her best efforts, her foot slipped and reflexively she tried to dig into the sliding rock. The whole mass of rubble started moving underfoot in a miniature avalanche that carried her downward a dozen feet. She lunged laterally across the slope and then slid, face down, behind a pile of boulders.

28

The immediate aftermath of her fall was an eerie silence. Regaining her legs in a pivoting squat, Jessie swiftly checked her surroundings and heard a flurry of motion coming from out of Pritt's perch in the rocks. Alerted and on guard, he was approaching as stealthily as his bulk and thick boots would allow and was prepared to kill.

Jessie froze, holding her breath . . . until a glint of metal caught in the golden blaze of early afternoon sun. Quickly she moved as a crack between the boulders came alive with lead. Pritt had seen her and had her in range. Jessie lay for a moment, sizing up a spot behind the rocks, then started crawling down. This brought her nearer to Pritt, but the rocks were bigger and gave better protection.

She found a deep niche when she came to a frost-split rock. Peering between its sharply divided sections, Jessie had a good perspective of the slope around her. Pritt came into view, then dipped from her field of vision. Apparently Biggs had spotted the fat blond man as well, for the dull boom of his rifle abruptly reverberated from the sandbar below. Pritt responded with a fast spray from his carbine. Bullets whined close to Jessie, kicking up slivers of chipped rock dust, but Pritt was shooting wildly, not knowing where Jessie was.

Then, in the sharply outlined section within her view, Pritt reappeared, weaving and ducking, running toward her. Gripping the knife tightly, Jessie slid the ball of her left thumb lightly over its blade and wished she could throw it. But the knife was fashioned more like a cutlass than a dagger; it was good for stabbing, slashing, perhaps even chopping, but not for tossing.

Pritt lumbered between the rocks, having difficulty

29

maintaining his balance on the pebbled slope as he checked right and left. He looked right when he should have looked left because Jessie was there, leaping, jabbing toward his eyes to shock him, to intimidate him into surrender.

"Drop the gun!" she snapped loudly. "Don't move!"

Pritt was indeed shocked. Gawking, he jerked spasmodically, slipped on the gravel, and out of sheer luck and desperation managed to parry her thrust with his carbine. Jessie missed his face, but not by much. She could actually see his flesh go gray with fear, even as he swiftly recovered and aimed at her.

"Shit! I'll blow your head off for this!"

He was fast, but not fast enough. Already Jessie was dropping to one knee, her other leg outstretched, in a countering maneuver that brought her inside the arc of his swiveling carbine. Springing up, she clamped the deflected barrel with her left hand and yanked it toward her, while bringing the knife ripping across Pritt's front. The blade tore open his shirt at the collar and made a slender gash diagonally from breastbone to ribs, before slicing through the thick muscles of Pritt's forearm. The wounded outlaw wavered, his carbine falling from nerveless fingers.

"I mean business," Jessie stated. "I want some answers."

Stunned, Pritt stared with bulging eyes. Something about his stare stopped Jessie cold, for she had seen that expression before. It was the look of a man facing death. The next instant, Jessie knew why. Pritt reached toward his throat, and just before his fingers covered his neck, she saw a flap of skin fall away and a spitting cloud of blood erupt. She had reacted defensively, hastily, her knife thrust not only cutting his chest and arm, but inadvertently slashing his throat before that.

Pritt tried to stem the tidal wave of crimson with his fingers, but it didn't work. The liquid oozed around his hands, turning his front into a sodden scarlet mess in seconds. As Jessie watched, he fell back, seemingly in slow motion, and tumbled down the slope, bounced off a ledge, and landed near the riverbank.

Sickened, disgusted, Jessie turned away. "Hell!"

Quickly hiking back to Pritt's horse, she found the saddlebags stuffed with currency, most of it large denomination greenbacks bound in bank wrappers. She didn't stop to count it, convinced it was the amount that the Sacramento fence had paid Pritt for the stolen bonds. She rebuckled the bags and rode the horse down into the grove of trees fringing the riverbank. There she dismounted, stripped the gear off the horse, and slapped it across its rump, sending it on its way.

She left the cash in the saddlebags, figuring as she returned to the sandbar that the Biggses may be honorable folk, but a quarter of a million was a sore temptation, and the less said or shown the better. To her delight and vast relief, she saw Ki, walking toward her with a grin on his face, and Rachel, standing safely beside her uncle. Ki seized Jessie by the hand and escorted her back, where they all exchanged short accounts of their travails. Jessie traded Duncan his knife for her boots, which he had thoughtfully brought from the ferry.

While she was putting them on, he declared, "Well now, Jessie—after such a to-do, callin' you Jessie ain't bein' too familiar, is it?—it goes without sayin' that me'n Rachel owe you'n Ki our lives. It's powerful peculiar, though."

Jessie smiled briefly and then tried to divert any questions of his by asking, "Do you think maybe this was an

31

attempt to get you, Duncan? I mean, do your brother and father have any enemies out here who might object to you and Rachel coming to Oregon?"

"I ain't got the slightest notion why that man cut us adrift," Duncan answered, shaking his head. "M'brother Thurlow once wrote that this country swarmed with no-good'ns, so p'raps it was a holdup try. Or somebody after the ferryman, wanting to kill him and wreck his boat. I 'fess neither makes much sense, though."

Rachel's eyes flashed angrily. "You're right, Uncle Dunc. A robber would have a terrible time collecting any loot, and why would someone with a grudge against the ferryman want to kill four innocent travelers to boot? I suspect there's more to it."

Ki, having caught Jessie's intentions, gave a big shrug and sighed. "If there is, it's a mystery the fat, blond guy isn't about to solve for us. Instead of chewing on a bone, suppose we try to get your wagon off the ferry."

This task was simpler than they had dared hope. There was only a ten-inch drop from the grounded end of the scow to the firm footing of the sandbar, and the ferryman had a portable ramp lashed to the bulwark. They used it to form a roadway for the wheels of the wagon.

When the wagon was safely ashore, Jessie pointed to a particular spot on the bank. "From what I saw, that patch there appears to have the easiest grade up to the top of the bank," she explained. "Your team should be able to pull it. Going along the edge after that might be a tight squeeze in spots, but with a little care, I think you'll make the road. Keep on it, and you'll reach Grants Pass in no time."

"Appreciate the advice," Duncan replied, beginning to unharness his team. "I reckon we'll rest here a spell, and then head on to my paw's cabin, which is northeast, not west, of here."

"Y'mean, toward Sweetgum?"

Duncan nodded. "Accordin' to his directions, his place is right on the way. If he'n Thurlow ain't there now, it stands to reason they'll return there eventually, so we'll wait for 'em."

Rachel, who was unloading some pots and pans from the wagon, called out, "Uncle Dunc, invite our friends for a late lunch with us."

"Thanks, but we should be going." Jessie mounted her horse and glanced knowingly at Ki. "We've got a long trek ahead of us."

"Right." Ki had recovered his and Jessie's lariats and was tying his to his pommel. "Well, nice to have met you," he said to Duncan and Rachel. "Good luck."

Rachel waved gaily. "Don't forget next week!"

"Next week?" Jessie asked.

Ki shifted uncomfortably. "Forget it. Just an idea."

"Uh-huh, just a little something we got straight between us," Rachel added, giggling. "It's not important. Easy come, easy go."

"Stifle your joshing, gal," Duncan told his niece with perplexed annoyance, and he regarded Jessie gravely. "I'd be obliged if you'd pass on a word about us, Jessie, if'n you chance across my paw or brother. They're of my size an' looks, 'cept Paw is pure bald."

Jessie nodded. "We'd be happy to. Adiós!"

She led the way as they rode across the sandbar and up the bank. Plunging into the timber to retrieve Pritt's saddlebags, she turned to Ki, who was a pace behind, and clucked her tongue.

"You ought to be ashamed of yourself."

33

"What?"

"I don't know how you do it. And with such a sweet girl, too."

"Rachel? Now, wait—"

"It's scandalous. You must've caught her from behind, Ki, that's the only explanation. You got her when her back was turned . . ."

Chapter 4

They rode upriver to the northern ferry landing, Jessie's horse now weighted down by the cash-bloated saddle-bags. Passing the big timbers that had supported the ferry cables, they noticed the stubs of four-inch hemp hawser and an axe lying in the nearby weeds where Pritt had discarded it after setting the ferry adrift.

"One problem gone," Jessie remarked, patting a saddlebag.

"Do we head back or look into the other one?"

"Well, we have to go out of our way to get across the Rogue again, Ki, so we might as well go out of our way by way of Emerald. I think we should check the situation while we're in the vicinity."

They took the main road at a spritely trot and pretty soon came to a fork. A weathered signpost had arrows that pointed in each direction, GRANTS PASS to the left on the main road and SWEETGUM to the right on a deep-rutted, secondary wagon trail. They struck out on the trail to Sweetgum, the route which the Biggses would also be traveling, unsure where exactly the Emerald Timber Company was located, yet confident they could gain directions once they reached Sweetgum.

35

The trail was definitely not the shortest link between two places, for it unraveled cross-country through a series of canyons, dips, and switchback grades. For hours they followed the meandering route. The sun was nearing the conifer-clad heights of the Coast Range behind them when they emerged on a plateau and were startled by a high-pitched scream wafting through the timber ahead of them.

Jessie stiffened. "A cougar?"

"Cougars don't scream this time of day," Ki responded, shaking his head. "Sounded more human to me, someone in bad pain."

The anguished cry carried to them again, choking off at the top of its crescendo and putting a chill down Jessie's spine. "No doubt about it, Ki, somebody's in trouble over yonder."

Kicking their mounts into a gallop, they dashed along the trail in search of the screamer. They were able to trace better when the agony sounded a third time, louder, from someplace close by but off the trail. Turning their horses, they moved single file along a meager path that marked an old Indian passage into the heart of a gulch. They forged through thick clumps of rhododendrons and hemlock scrub before finally reining in at the edge of a clearing.

A log cabin squatted in the center of the clearing, with a wisp of smoke squirreling from its crude, rock chimney. Two horses were grazing beyond the cabin. From within echoed another shriek—and they knew instantly now that someone inside was in the throes of some misery.

Jessie and Ki spurred forward, the strike of their horses' hooves ringing on the rock slabs of the clearing floor. The front door was on the far side of the cabin, and only a narrow window broke the log face of the wall the two

36

riders were approaching. The barrel of a rifle suddenly jutted from that window.

Ki yelled a warning and flung himself from his saddle, even as flame spat from the rifle bore and a bullet drilled the space where Ki had been an instant before. Jessie wheeled and dashed into the sheltering timber; Ki sprinted for the cover of a nearby boulder. A second slug from the cabin laced grit in his face as he dived behind the rock, palming *shuriken* from his vest.

Having taken the precaution of reloading her revolver, Jessie triggered at the window from the concealment of the brush. Her shots only seemed to provoke those inside, a volley of lead from the rifle—a Henry repeater by its look and action—whipping the air, earth, and foliage around her. But Ki launched *shuriken* through the glassless window with a more telling effect.

"Whazzat? Yeow!" one voice barked.

"Holy she-it!" another yowled.

The next instant booted feet drummed across the front porch. From their cover, neither Jessie nor Ki could glimpse the two horses at the other edge of the clearing, but they could hear a pounding of hoofbeats as two riders left the clearing and tore off through the concealing brush and trees. Cautiously Jessie circled around and gathered their horses, leading them back into cover. Ki crouched behind his boulder for a full minute before stepping into the open. He was still wary.

"Cover me," he called to Jessie, "I'll check the cabin."

Jessie's answer sounded from the backdrop of the forest. With his fingers stroking the knife sheathed at his waist, Ki sprinted across the clearing and gained the shelter of the log wall.

From the cabin interior filtered the sound of a man's raucous, spongy breathing, interspersed with groans. A

37

crunch of gravel startled Ki and he wheeled, then relaxed, as he saw that Jessie had followed him, poised alert.

"Curious, eh?" he chided. "It killed the cat, you know."

Together they ducked around the corner where the chimney stood. The smell of dust floated into the clearing from the gulch beyond, indicating a pell-mell getaway on horseback. Gingerly they moved on, rounding the next corner and stepping up on a small front porch. The cabin door hung open on its hinges, and from within came a smell of scorched flesh, bacon grease, powder-smoke, and untanned hides. In short, it reeked to high heaven.

Ki went first, standing framed on the threshold and raking the dark interior with widening eyes. Jessie pressed alongside, and as her pupils adjusted to the gloom, she gasped in horror.

A bald oldster, stripped nude, sat writhing in ropes that bound him to a chair in front of the fireplace. His aged body was welted with ugly blisters. One glance at the sizzling hot poker jutting from the embers on the hearth told of the torment to which the old man had been subjected.

Holstering her pistol, Jessie strode across the floor and laid a hand sympathetically on the victim's shoulder. The man shuddered in violent recoil, moans whining from his flaccid mouth. Ki, whipping out his knife, severed the rawhide thongs that tied the man to the chair and, with Jessie, caught him before he could pitch to the floor. Gently they lifted their frail burden and carried him across the room to a bunk.

"He needs a doctor, Ki, and fast."

"Maybe there's one in Sweetgum."

"There must be," Jessie insisted plaintively. "Will you . . . ?"

"Like the wind. I'll ride there straight as I can, and not by that drunken snake of a road," Ki added as he headed out the door. "I'll be back with a doctor just as quickly as I can."

A moment later Jessie heard Ki's roan heading up the path. It was then she noticed that the old man was opening his eyes for the first time. They were the staring, blank orbs of a person driven insane by unendurable agonies, and they regarded Jessie with a wild intensity that was pitiful to see.

Glancing about the cabin for something—anything— that might help him, Jessie saw that the walls were hung with a variety of animal traps, and a nearby corner was piled high with pelts baled for shipping. This was a trapper's home. This realization, coupled with the old man's total baldness, struck a chord in Jessie's memory.

"Would you be Zachary Biggs?" she asked, but got no reply.

She found a jug of whiskey on the fireplace mantel and brought it to the bunk, giving the man a long swig of the raw, fiery liquor. Emitting a slavering moan then, he managed to bring his eyes into focus—a focus that reflected approaching death. Feebly he croaked for another snort and then tried to speak.

"They was tryin' . . . force me to tell where . . . where me'n my boy hid our skins," the trapper gasped falteringly. "Goin' to kill me . . . same's they did Thurlow last winter . . . Rich cache, huge . . ."

Nausea assailed Jessie as she thought how hard this oldster was struggling, how hard he was dying. His flesh was charred in a multitude of places, even in his groin, with deep burns made by the red-hot poker. The pulse in his withered wrists was erratic, ebbing. This was Duncan Biggs' father, of that she was positive. His references to "my boy" and "Thurlow" were proof of that.

"Listen, Zack!" she whispered urgently, giving the trapper a third pull on the whiskey jug. "You've got to hang on. Your son Duncan and granddaughter Rachel from Indiana are on their way here."

Zachary Biggs' eyes revolved in their sockets, the bootleg whiskey having taken hold of him and rousing his flagging vitality. But when he spoke again, it was incoherent, the gibberish of delirium.

"Secret of . . . of beaver cache . . . in Thurlow's brain," he muttered, his arms and legs threshing on the hide blanket under him. "Wapato Gorge . . . Silver skull . . . Didn't blab this time . . ."

A paroxysm wracked the trapper's naked form, and his convulsing muscles suddenly went limp. Jessie leaned over him, thumbing a eyelid, then bent an ear to his still chest. Zack Biggs had found the peace of death.

Saddened, Jessie began wrapping the body in a robe.

She was almost finished when a shadow fell across the floor. She whirled about, hand stabbing for her pistol— then pausing, freezing, as she saw it was too late. Two men loomed in the doorway, each with a Colt .45 jutting from a fist and trained on her. On one of them glinted a marshal's badge.

"Heist 'em, gal!" the lawman ordered gruffly. "Females are deadlier'n males, I know, so don't think you can put the vamp on me."

Slowly Jessie lifted her arms, her eyes appraising them both carefully. The lawman was of medium size and height and displayed a prosperity unusual for his profession, what with trousers of a fine light wool, polished hussar boots, and a diamond pinky ring. He also exuded a certain arrogance, his jutting jaw smoothly shaven to the roots of a heavy beard that gave his face a blue-black cast. His companion wore common range garb, rumpled and dirty, and had cold, predatory features—a vulture's curved beak for a nose and a gashlike mouth under the awning of a gray mustache.

"I'm Marshal Freis," the lawman announced, crossing to lift Jessie's pistol from her holster. "Just you keep my star in mind, if you start to get uppity notions. Bruno, what's inside that robe?"

The other man—a deputy, Jessie presumed—folded back the robe. "Why, it's Zack!" he growled hoarsely, leaning closer, nostrils twitching from the odor of scorched flesh. "Been tortured real bad, and is deader'n a mackerel. Looks like maybe we got here in time to nab Zack's killer smack-dab after the act."

"That's not true! Marshal, I was trying to save him. The men who did that to Zack Biggs fled into the woods only minutes ago."

"Uh-huh. And just for the record, who are you?"

"Starbuck. Jessica Starbuck."

"*The* Starbuck?" Deputy Bruno blurted. "Jeez, I've gandered stories about you in the weeklies, on how you're rich and famous."

Marshal Freis gave a sardonic laugh. "Don't be dumb, Bruno. D'you imagine a high society belle who's used to hob-nobbin' with kings and industrialists would be here? Wearin' jeans and a gun and looking like she was dunked wet and left out to dry?"

"You'd better believe it," Jessie snapped, growing nettled.

"I'm inclined to believe what I see, gal. And what I see is more on the lines of a country hussy," Freis retorted. "Bruno, her horse must be outside. Fetch it and check her belongings for a name."

"Yeah, I'll see if I can find out who she actually is,"

the deputy agreed, hurrying out the door.

Jessie eyed Freis darkly. "You're making a big mistake."

"If I am, I'll apologize." Freis reached in a pocket and fished out a pair of handcuffs. Swiftly the manacles were clamped over Jessie's wrists, pinning her arms behind her back. "It's well known that Zack Biggs and his son trapped a wealth o' prime beaver last winter," he declared, holstering his Colt and sitting in the chair that Zack had been tied to. "Thurlow and the skins dropped from sight sometime back then—Thurlow likely waylaid and done in, like Zack always claimed. Anyhow, him an' the pelts ain't showed in public ever since. Ain't hard to figure that some folks would think the pelts were hidden and Zack knew where, and they would come try to force the old guy into telling."

"That's right. That's exactly what those men were doing."

"Uh-huh. Amazin' how you're here and the men ain't."

"V–Vince!" Deputy Bruno lurched inside, stuttering with excitement as he waved a sheath of bills. "M–money! Her bags are stuffed to burstin'!"

Marshal Freis frowned menacingly at Jessie. "Well, that settles it. Zack already cashed in the pelts, probably at Grants Pass where an opportunin' woman like you would've met up with him. You followed him here, and when your wicked wiles and his whiskey didn't work, you used that poker on him. Then you robbed him and murdered him just afore you were gonna escape. The evidence is all here."

"I tell you, you're wrong! We were passing when we heard—"

"We?"

"A friend. He's gone to Sweetgum for a doctor."

42

Freis turned to his deputy. "Did you see anyone on the road?"

"You know I didn't, Vi—I mean, Marshal. We was together."

"Uh-huh, and there weren't nobody we passed en route here." Freis rose to his feet, drawing his revolver. "Come along, whoever you are. If you do have an accomplice lurking somewhere, be warned that you'll get the first of any shots fired."

"But—"

"Nope, I don't want to listen to no more lies." He gestured toward the door. "Me'n the coroner will come back for Zack's body and the evidence. You'll get your chance to speak in court."

Her handcuffed arms held impotently behind her, Jessie stepped out into the sunlight. She saw two horses near the porch and instantly recognized them as the same mounts which Zack Biggs' killers had ridden. Jessie's lips compressed with dismay. She would receive no mercy from this so-called peace officer and his deputy. They were setting her up!

Awkwardly she climbed astride her horse, Bruno covering her at pointblank range while the marshal stepped into his saddle. Then Bruno mounted and the two corrupt lawmen, bracketing their prisoner between them, headed away from the cabin toward the road to Sweetgum.

Jessie rode in grim silence, reflecting on the tragic discovery which Duncan and Rachel would make when they arrived . . . and on her own plight that could readily result in a hangman's noose. Her one ray of hope was Ki.

Chapter 5

Ki was deep in the wooded plateau country footing the
Cascade Range, riding as swiftly yet judiciously as he
could toward Sweetgum. Or so he hoped. He had a keen
sense of direction and felt he was generally following a
line that would bring him to the small logging town, but
the terrain kept growing harsher with thickening stands
of timber and steepening escarpments gashed by numer-
ous chasms. And the light was dying. Increasingly he
was unable to see the westering sun itself, only the red-
smeared horizon above the Coast Range far behind him.

At one point he reached a local summit, a stone-
slabbed ledge from which he could survey the wild expanse of rocks, forests, and canyons that stretched before
him. On his left he spotted the meandering wagon road
he'd purposely avoided, and to his relief, in the distance
ahead he glimpsed Sweetgum, lying beneath a blue haze
of smoke from its mill. Carefully he took his bearings,
allowing his horse a brief rest. It and Jessie's horse had
been borrowed from a Starbuck company in Sacramento,
and although far from being spirited thoroughbreds, both
mounts had proven to be dependable workers, trained
well and evenly disposed.

45

He pushed on confidently. Even so, he had to rein in a few times to scrutinize the deceiving perspectives, and twice, much to his annoyance, he had to correct for having strayed. Shortly, while bottoming a ridge, he chanced upon a minor wagon trail. It was scarcely more than a narrow ribbon where passing hooves and wheels had chewed the ground raw, yet it angled more or less the right way and was better than a path forged solely in his head, so he decided to try it for a while.

Turning, Ki jiggered his roan into a trot. The trail plowed through brush and gulches and flinty hogbacks, eventually entering a dense forest of cathedral-size trees. The route was now marked by indigo and burgundy shadows. Ki maintained a steady pace, pleased that he was still heading on course—or as much on course as the jagged, hemmed-in landscape would allow.

Then, rounding an unusually sharp bend, he found himself confronted by a fallen Douglas fir, its mammoth trunk blocking the trail. Ordinarily he wouldn't have felt concern, rotten and wind-toppled trees being a natural enough hazard. But back in the undergrowth, the exposed stump and the sawdust mounds around it showed a fresh yellow color, indicating this fir had been recently felled with the express intention of barring passage. The reason was scrawled on a makeshift signboard spiked against the trunk:

STAY OUT! THIS MEANS YOU!
PROPERTY CLOSED AND PATROLLED BY ARMED GUARDS!
ALL CATTLEMEN AND OTHER TRESPASSERS WILL BE SHOT!
—EMERALD TIMBER CO.

Ki's obsidian eyes narrowed as he considered the blunt warning. "Cattlemen" undoubtedly referred to the Bar M in particular and evidently matters had gotten worse than Jessie knew. He himself wasn't rigged out as a cowboy, but he was wearing the sort of casual range garb that might cause a nervous sentry to make a fatal mistake. In any case, he was definitely a stranger—at least until he could introduce himself—and if that sign was to be believed, he wouldn't be given much of a chance to.

Yet he simply didn't have time to backtrack to the sinuous road or to detour around sixty sections of timberland. Jessie and that oldster were counting on him to bring a doctor; he had to reach Sweetgum by the most direct route, and that meant crossing Emerald property for some distance. And he had to be quick about it.

Mentally bracing himself against ambushing gunfire, Ki touched the flanks of his roan and veered around the fallen tree. No shots came, but he remained in the perpetual twilight of the conifers, avoiding thickets and keeping to the sound-deadening carpet of needles as much as possible.

He was riding like this when he came to a logged-off clearing several acres in extent, and he caught sight of a horse grazing at the base of a tall pine. He reined in by an edge of the clearing, his eyes peering about and then scanning upwards to the top of the pine. It had been stripped of its branches, its crown hacked off by an ax a fair two hundred feet above the forest floor. At its cropped peak, a rigger was hanging by his lifebelt and spurs as he busily installed a steel collar to the crown.

The horse, of course, belonged to the rigger. And the pine, Ki realized, was being made into a spar tree, the collar to serve as an anchor for a steel cable—a high line—that would be used to drag heavy logs to a holding pond or wherever.

Ki hesitated, partly out of fascination for the rigger's

dangerous task, and partly out of confusion about how he was going to cross the clearing without the rigger's spotting him. A soft rustling of foliage at the other end of the open field caused him to shift his gaze. He waited, peering, and was about to chalk it to some small animal, when a skulking figure emerged from a patch of brambles and stealthily approached the spar tree.

The man's furtiveness and his haste as he wedged a brick-size package into a niche between two roots told Ki that he also wished to avoid being seen by the rigger. He appeared to be a tall bruiser, and although he wore some attire favored by lumberjacks, buckaroo was written all over him—over his wide-brim hat, his holstered revolver, his pointy boots with their long-shanked California spurs. When the man scurried back under cover, Ki was better able to gauge his great shoulders, lean thighs, and saddle-warped legs, telltale signs of a long-time stock rider.

For long minutes after the man vanished as silently as he had come, Ki took care not to make any move. High overhead the rigger cursed, his tools ringing erratically and winking in the last light of the sunset. Ki could hear axes and saws filtering rhythmically from somewhere far off, interspersed with the remote thunder of crashing trees. Restless to be on his way again and suspecting the stranger was gone, Ki finally eased back and started skirting the field.

He just about got to the brambles when a violent explosion erupted close by, its blinding shock wave nearly throwing him off his horse. Instantly it was followed by mushrooming clouds of black smoke, dust, and splintered wood. Reeling, fighting to control his roan, Ki hazily perceived that the blast had originated at the base of the spar tree, and that now, sheared of support, the giant

48

pine was slowly keeling over.

At its crown, the rigger was sailing this shattered tree to the ground. Stunned and struggling aboard his bucking horse, Ki could only watch helplessly as the rigger made a wild grab for the steel collar he had been fitting to the top. The rigger's bellowing scream of terror sounded above the deep *whoosh* the tree emitted as it plummeted through space. It landed with a quake that reverberated through the depths of the forest.

Ki leaped from the saddle, snagging his reins on some branches to keep his horse from bolting, and thrust head-long through the brambles toward the downed tree. He glimpsed the stranger farther back in the timber, mounting a mare. So filled with fury was Ki that for a second he turned from the clearing to pursue the man, who had lurked close to see how well his little surprise package worked. Before Ki could do more than turn, the man disappeared at a gallop into the forest shadows.

That blink of a moment had been enough for Ki's honed vision to memorize two facts. One was the killer's most distinguishing feature, a burst tomato of a nose mashed crooked against the right side of his face. The other was his horse's brand, a Bar M seared on its rump.

Pivoting, Ki again set out across the field, aware the rigger could not possibly have survived, yet determined to get to him in case of a miracle. He dashed through the brush and followed the felled tree for a hundred feet to its crown, where the rigger sprawled grotesquely, pinioned by his lifebelt and climbing spurs. As expected, he was mortally injured, and Ki, hunkering alongside, was astounded to find he still had a few breaths left in his smashed body. The rigger's eyes fluttered and he stared venomously at Ki. He strained to force words through his shattered mouth.

"You hafta kill . . . every Emerald jack to win this . . . feud, cowboy," the rigger managed, choking. "Bar M . . . pay for this."

Ki tried to respond, to comfort and explain, but it was futile. Almost immediately the mangled rigger relaxed and expired.

Frustrated, exasperated, Ki paused crouching. "Damn! First at the cabin and now here with this poor guy—a shade too late each time," Ki muttered, shaking his head. "Well, I'd best get moving. No use lingering and asking for more trouble, when maybe I can still do some good for that old fellow."

Before Ki could act, his ears caught a thrashing in the brush. Thinking perhaps the killer was trying to sneak back and silence him, the only witness, Ki sprang and whirled, his hands digging for weapons. Then came the voices of men shouting and swearing and clomps of boots running along the fallen tree. Ki froze as he saw he was surrounded by eight towering lumberjacks armed with felling axes and hickory-handled peavies.

"Wait!" Ki called. "Hold it!"

The jacks were of no mind to. "Get him!" one bellowed and they converged, their expressions hard and angry.

Ki knew he was in for it. He couldn't defend himself effectively without maiming and possibly killing, yet this misguided mob was comprised of Emerald men, Starbuck men, whom he couldn't rightly blame for feeling enraged. On the other hand, he wasn't about to let them beat or stomp or chop him to a bloody pulp.

Gauging the swarming assault, Ki was the first to attack. He lashed high with a leaping kick, tempering its normally fatal force, wishing only to incapacitate. He caught the nearest man in the solar plexus, landed, and

50

kicked again, this time his slipper scooping dirt and spraying it into the faces of two other men. The first man was falling to his knees, clutching his belly; the second pair pawed grit out of their eyes and blindly swung their peavies; the rest of the jacks tackled Ki in a pile, grabbing his legs and arms and pounding him with ax handles.

Ki resisted, using elbow smashes, kicks, punches, and open-handed strikes and managing to be quite effective. But there were too many of them, and though they howled and went skidding aside, they'd blearily recover and pounce back into the fray. They smashed his ribs and battered his face and kept trying to break his bones with their heavy boots. Still Ki struggled, wishing he could resist completely and lay waste to these brawlers and grimly enduring the pain as he battled to remain upright.

The odds took their toll. Handles and fists kept hammering, hammering, driving Ki to his knees. He bucked against the jacks as they strove to keep him down, then a well-aimed peavy handle struck the back of his head, and again, harder. Ki dropped flat on his face and figured he'd better lie down until his wits returned.

The jacks drew back. All except one fingered bruises and loose teeth, Ki perceived woozily through slitted eyes. A husky young man with a rust-colored beard suddenly hefted his peavy and lunged as if intending to harpoon Ki.

Ki tensed, but just as he was about to counter the hurtling stab, a barrel-chested jack in a plaid shirt and high-laced boots dived at the youth. "Drop it, Shaw!" the big man roared, grappling the youth to the ground and wrestling away the peavy.

"Get off me! Give that back, Hans Aubrecht!" the young logger ranted. "This shit murdered my brother! He murdered Leroy!"

"Easy, Gerry, easy! Liable he did, and if this is the kind of tactics McManus aims to use on us, he'll sure find out that Emerald can play the game against the Bar M. But that ain't no call for you killin' a man who's unarmed and nearly unconscious! Boys, give me a hand."

The other loggers stepped in to help the man called Aubrecht control Gerry Shaw. The berserk youth struggled, raving, "Maybe you are foreman and I gotta take your orders about work, but this here is personal! I ain't stoppin' till I've settled with Bar M!"

"Enough of such talk!" Aubrecht snarled loudly to quash any seeds of mutiny before they could sprout. He straightened, a Nordic giant whose build sealed his authority over his crew. "We're taking the cowboy and your brother to camp, and leavin' any killin' for the boss lady to decide," he stated, dusting his pants. Then he crossed to the corpse of the rigger and reverently doffed his cap.

His crew filed after and grouped around, Gerry Shaw now in a state of abject grief. Aubrecht raked a big hand through his tangled brown hair. "This's a wretched price to pay for defendin' our timber claim, but Leroy will be avenged, Gerry, don't worry. I reckon Miz Gideon will call for that gent to be stretched on a handy snag and left for McManus to come cut down."

Sobbing, Gerry Shaw released his brother from the lifebelt. Leroy's horse had been blown to shreds, so Ki's roan was used to carry the broken body. Ki was rousted with slaps and shakes, and he came to, though he feigned grogginess and suffered a ferocious headache. Aubrecht kept him within arm's reach, walking slightly in back and to the left of Ki. The other loggers, grim with the shock of this tragedy, retrieved their axes and peavies and trudged behind.

Chapter 6

The sullen procession continued to thread doggedly through the deep timber. Some of the jacks took to glaring and muttering threats at Ki, but as long as Aubrecht commanded the situation, Ki felt in no immediate danger.

For that he was gratified, but it scarcely helped him get on with his mission, nor would relating his story help much now. Somehow he doubted he'd be believed. Once at the camp he'd be able to tell Mrs. Gideon who he was and how he needed a doctor and had witnessed the rigger's death. If things went well, he'd be sent on his way. If not, he'd probably be held until Jessie was located and his identity confirmed. If things went as sour as they had so far ... He didn't want to think about that.

Along the way, Ki caught the sound of water cascading down a rocky gorge. He figured that would be the Rogue tributary, the center of the Emerald–Bar M controversy in the increasingly vicious timber-cattle feud.

The journey ended at a flat mountain meadow that was bisected by a rushing brook. Next to the brook was a group of log buildings: bunkhouses, a cookhouse, a cache house, a wagon shack, and a corraled stable all forming a sort of street. Set apart on a slight knoll was a bungalow that served, Ki knew, as the manager's living quarters and company office. At a distance he could see a small mill and drying sheds outlined dimly by the first glimmers of moonlight.

Lamps burned in the bungalow and a couple of the bunkhouses. As Ki and the loggers approached the camp, a billow of sparks rose from the cookhouse stovepipe, indicating someone had just added wood to the fire.

Then angling toward the bungalow, Aubrecht cupped his hands and hailed his boss, "Miz Gideon! Hey, Miz Gideon! Bar M's answered your warnin' sign on Trail Six! Blasted Six's new spar tree and killed the rigger!"

The door of the bungalow swept open and Margot Gideon hurried down to meet them. She was dressed in trousers, low-heeled boots, a mackinaw, and a logger's cap, but despite her rough clothes she was very definitely a woman. About five feet seven and in her mid-thirties, she was no hothouse beauty—her black hair was a bit frizzled, and her face was lined by years of toil. Yet her face also showed character, her lips full and her black eyes alert, and her figure curved in where it should and out where it should with undeniable appeal. Under different circumstances, Ki decided, she'd be an interesting person to get to know.

As it was, Ki saw Margot's face pale as she strode to his horse and looked at Leroy Shaw's mangled remains. After a brief conference with Aubrecht, which was too low-pitched for Ki to hear, she turned her attention to him.

"Just answer two things, stranger," she said in a tone that could've etched crystal. "Who are you? And who hired you to kill my rigger this afternoon, Liam McManus or Vincent Freis?"

His skull still throbbing, Ki groped to an upturned

keg and sat rubbing his bloody face and hair. Finally he said, "My name is Ki. Nobody hired me because I'm not the one who did it."

"Ki?" Margot frowned quizzically. "Sounds familiar..."

"I usually accompany Miss Jessica Starbuck."

"Our owner? You're not that Ki; you can't be!"

Ki indicated the roan. "Search my bags." While Aubrecht did just that, Ki stood and appeared to empty all his pockets. The result was inconclusive, for Ki was intentionally traveling light, and his effects were too few and impersonal to prove his identity.

"What little he's got he likely faked or stole," Gerry Shaw said. "Don't let him fool you. We caught him."

Margot nodded sagely and told Ki, "And you said yourself the real Ki is companion to Miss Starbuck. Where is she?"

"She's waiting for me to fetch a doctor," Ki replied, and he launched into a detailed account of rescuing the tortured oldster, of Jessie's dispatching him to Sweetgum, and his overland trek that had brought him to the clearing where he had tarried until the explosion.

Margot listened intently, plainly striving to be fair in her judgment despite the seriousness of losing her rigger. After Ki finished, she asked him to describe the old man, and after he had, she turned to Aubrecht. "Zack Biggs, it must be."

The connection startled Ki, but Aubrecht merely scoffed. "So?"

"Hans, Miss Starbuck owns Emerald. She's going to be sore at us already without our making it worse!"

"Well, it's simple enough to check. I'll send someone to Biggs' cabin, and if the lady exists, he'll bring her back. But face it, if this guy didn't kill Leroy, who did?"

Ki said, "I don't know his name, but it was a Bar M rider."

Margot looked oddly disappointed. "Are you sure?"

"Bar M was the brand on his horse. I saw him hide a packet of blasting powder at the roots of the spar. I'd no idea what he was up to until he detonated it. When I saw the rigger fall, I rushed to help and that's why you found me there."

"Crap!" Gerry Shaw swore caustically. "You planted that charge and're lying to save your hide!" Blatantly losing control again, he wheeled on Margot. "His outfit ain't Bar M, and his horse ain't Bar M branded. What the devil do you expect after having us post signs warning Bar M we'll shoot all hands? Naturally that bastard McManus would import a stranger to attack us. You're deep in a war and you know it, but won't admit it!"

Stepping up, Aubrecht slapped Gerry hard across the face with the back of his hand. But Margot shook her head slowly, refusing to take offense at the abusive tirade.

"Put Ki or whoever he is in the feed shed and lock him in under guard," she ordered Aubrecht. "We'll know more after we've checked his story, maybe enough to get to the bottom of this."

Gerry rubbed his stinging mouth, and when he spoke again, his voice was controlled and determined. "Nothing's gonna keep me from settlin' the score. This slant-eyed varmint is soon gonna swing."

"If he's the killer, he'll be punished," Margot vowed. "But we must learn all about who hired him before going off and lynching him. Someone may be a lot guiltier than he is."

Without further discussion, Aubrecht and a trio of jacks escorted Ki to a small shed behind the cookhouse. Inside, Aubrecht lit a hanging lantern and told Ki, "Try

56

to escape by settin' the place afire, and it'll be your cooked goose." Then he left.

The door was closed and barred. Through its thick planks, Ki heard Aubrecht instruct the guard, "Stay put, Maxwell, stay sharp and stay awake. I'll have Calvert relieve you at one."

"Don't worry. I ain't rarin' to let our caged lobo catch me asleep. I still ache aplenty from where he whomped me afore."

"I'm worried less by him trying to bust out than by Gerry and his pals trying to bust in and string him from a rafter."

After that it fell quiet. By the dim glow from the lantern's soot-fouled chimney, Ki began to survey his eight-by-eight prison. Evidently it was the cook's supply dump, for much of it was filled with burlap sacks and squat barrels containing flour, cereal, and other bulk foods. There were no windows, the walls were of solid logs, and the floor was impregnable bedrock under a silting of dirt. For a cell, the shed wasn't too shabby.

Ki supposed that he could manage to break out. The instincts of a trapped man goaded him to ponder how, but nothing came readily to mind that wouldn't create a serious ruckus. But since he basically just had to wait for Jessie, he decided to relax and await further developments.

He settled on a bag of oatmeal and purposely slowed his breathing. He crossed his arms and cupped his hands over his ears. To many his posture would look strange and uncomfortable: to Ki it was a vital position for focusing internal energies and reviving intrinsic health and strength.

He remained thus when the door opened.

Margot entered and stopped short. "Are you ill?"

57

"Meditating."

"Oh. I . . . Would you care to clean up?"

"Thanks." Ki straightened and took the soap, wash-rag, and basin of water she was carrying. "You did send someone, didn't you?"

"Of course, and another man to fetch Doc Harn there, too." Then she said, as Ki was lathering, "I want you to describe fully that Bar M man. Don't fib, now. The answer is very important to me."

"I barely glimpsed him," Ki replied, but while scrubbing, he told Margot all he could recall, including the skewed tomato nose.

Margot thought, quirking her lips. "I'm sure I know by sight every Bar M hand, and this man doesn't fit any of the crew."

"He fit a Bar M horse just fine. Y'know, when I told you he was a Bar M rider, you reacted almost crestfallen. Now you seem almost relieved. Why're you reluctant to believe he is?"

"I'm not. Maybe he is, or maybe you're a liar—and the killer. What I doubt is Bar M being behind the sneak attack because whoever's responsible must be a devious schemer. And Liam McManus is blunt and windy with no more sly cunning than an elephant's foot."

"Well, he's shrewd enough to tie Emerald up in court."

"That's more Vince Freis' canniness than McManus'."

"Freis. You asked if I'd been hired by him, too."

Margot nodded. "If you don't know already, Vince Fries is a lawyer who got himself appointed our local state marshal. He's handling Bar M's suit and goes there quite a bit. Another of his clients is the cow syndicate that sold McManus the land. So he's got motive against us and access to Bar M horses—and he's crafty. If you're telling me the truth, it helps bear out my hunch that Freis

58

is more likely to be behind this than McManus."

A lanky man stepped in just then; he was laden with a steaming coffee pot and a tray of dishes heaped with potatoes, biscuits, and boiled pot roast. His grimy apron and hat branded him as the camp cook, and when he roughly set his load down, he glanced about scowling as though suspecting Ki of having swiped some of his stored foodstuffs.

"There's his snack like you ordered, Boss," he grumbled, "though why this skunk is still in eatin' condition is beyond me. If I'd had some arsenic, dang if I wouldn't have laced his grub."

Margot flushed indignantly. "I'll thank you to keep your opinions private, Cookie, and a civil tongue in your head."

"Don't bother to fire me 'cause I quit! Leroy's only the first victim, and there'll be more, many more. I'm leaving before the Bar M and your guest here bury me, too!"

The cook stalked out, slamming the door behind him, leaving Margot agape and Ki tersely aggravated. In the space of a few hours, Emerald had lost two of its most valuable crewmen—a rigger by explosion and the camp cook by resignation.

"My crew is in a rash mood," Margot said apologetically.

"As long as Gerry Shaw isn't posted to guard me, I think I'll be okay here till Jessie arrives. She shouldn't be much longer."

With a faint grin, Margot collected the basin, soap, and rag. Opening the door, she hesitated on the threshold and glanced back. "I don't understand it all," she said, her grin now a solicitous smile. "All I know is I hope you're Ki, and you won't have to hang."

59

Ki responded with a nod of agreement. He watched her move into the night, where the spread of feeble light revealed a big logger, a double-barrel shotgun cradled in his arm.

"Some of the boys might get nasty ideas, Maxwell."

"Depend on me, ma'am."

The door closed and Ki heard the heavy bar drop back into place. He went to the tray and coffeepot then, and though he had not eaten since morning, he dined leisurely, conscientiously savoring each bite. When finished, he formed a mattress out of burlap sacks. Weary and still suffering from the drubbing headache, Ki lay down to take a slight rest and promptly fell asleep.

His instincts estimated it was somewhat past midnight when he became aroused by a mutter of voices outside. He remained still and in a moment he could discern the conversing was merely between Maxwell and the guard named Calvert, who'd come to take the next shift of duty. They shot the bull while Maxwell smoked a cigarette. He then said good night, and Maxwell's receding bootsteps died away.

It was one or a little after.

And no Jessie.

Fully awake, Ki arose and began pacing, restless with concern and frustration. Jessie should have shown up by now. Yet he was stuck. There was nothing he could do, nowhere he could go, not one damn thing at all.

Well, there was one thing. The oil in the lantern was running low, and the wick was emitting choking fumes in the unventilated shed, so at least he could go blow it out before it snuffed him.

He was heading for the lantern when he heard Calvert's hoarse whisper: "It's clear, Gerry! C'mon!"

60

Ki stopped, a thin grin creasing his lips. Cautioning Margot not to post Shaw as his guard had been a bantering remark. Now his guard was selling out to the hot-tempered, grief-berserk youth.

Heavy boots grated on pebbled earth as several men stalked closer. Ki was facing the door with his hands out, fingers stiffened, his eyes gauging in anticipation, when it opened and Gerry Shaw stepped inside. Behind Shaw loomed other loggers—four, maybe five—bunched at the door, their faces contorted with hate.

"York got back from Biggs' place. Nobody home," Gerry snarled, leveling an old Remington .44 at Ki. "If you got any last lies, you better say 'em now 'cause in two seconds flat you'll be dancing the strangulation jig from one o' these rafters!"

Chapter 7

Unaware of Ki's misadventure, Jessie spent that afternoon riding handcuffed between Marshal Freis and Deputy Bruno. Their pace was steady and unhurried along the wagon road, which wound east and then north and vaguely followed the Rogue upstream. The river was often within earshot but never eyesight.

Along the first stretch, they passed a narrow lane that cut away to the left. Beside the lane was a large wooden signboard into which was carved the brand of the Bar M. Later on, while traversing the increasingly rugged foothills to the north, they crossed a plank bridge over the cataract-strewn gorge of a mountain river spilling down toward the Rogue. It was the disputed river, Jessie quickly realized, for spiked to a support post on the other side of the bridge was an old sawmill blade, on which was painted the name EMERALD and a hand whose finger pointed westward along a wagon trail.

Jessie now had a fairly good idea of how the Bar M and the Emerald lay in relation to each other. She made no mention of this or anything else to the lawmen. They were crooked as a dog's hind leg and would dispose of her in a flash if they ever knew the true situation. As long as they believed her to be some unknown tramp, they'd keep her alive to serve as their patsy for Zack Biggs' murder—and as long as she was alive, she had a chance of being rescued by Ki, or of being unshackled and gaining her derringer.

She hoped—indeed, half expected—Ki to intercept them while en route. When he hadn't by the time they breached the final rise, she began wondering what might have happened to him. They started down into the mountain-hemmed valley where Sweetgum nestled.

At a distance, the town appeared to be a motley hodge-podge of buildings, shacks, and tents, most of them strewn up across a shelf as protection against the flood-prone Rogue, which flowed a short distance beyond—past a pond, drying yard, and smoke-belching mill. Now, in late afternoon, the setting sun inflamed the Cascade peaks above the town and cast fiery streamers over the hill they were descending and radiated flashy hues off the waters of the churning river.

Jessie found Sweetgum bustling with eventide business. Yet the town exuded something else, a sense of menace that belied the honest activities of the teamsters, riders, and pedestrians who crowded its single main street. That feeling came from hombres with cold eyes and holsters, men who lounged with studied insolence against the saloon fronts. Gunhands. Jessie took note of their numbers, counting ten before she and the lawmen reined in by a squat structure between a mercantile and a feed store. Its lopsided sign and barred windows identified the building as Freis' office and jail.

Without delay, the marshal and his deputy hustled Jessie inside the office. While Bruno covered her with his pistol, Freis removed the handcuffs and locked her in the nearer of two cells. Then Freis hurried out and back with Jessie's saddlebags, which he stowed with her revolver in the bottom of his rifle cabinet. Satisfied, he drew out a sack of tobacco and a pipe.

"Make yourself comfy, gal. It won't be till tomorrow that you can plead your case afore our justice. He likes a good turn of ankle, so maybe you got a chance." Freis tamped his tobacco with his fingers and then cautioned, "Squawk about the money and it'll go worse for you. Stay mum, and I'll put in a good word."

"You're all heart."

"Ain't I, though!" Smirking, he drew a match and lit his pipe. "Well, we've got our duties to go do. Have you eaten?"

"Not since this morning."

"Bruno will fetch you grub later on." Tossing the keys to his deputy, who stuffed them in a back pocket, Freis nodded curtly to Jessie and joined Bruno at the door. "In the meantime, take a rest. You ain't going nowhere."

Bruno closed the door behind them. There was the sound of another key latching it—the rear door was already barred—and Jessie was left to her own dismal thoughts as she gazed around.

The office itself was a sty: a stove bulging with rubbish, reward posters tacked about like wallpaper, and the rifle cabinet empty save for one dusty shotgun and her belongings. The cell was small and held only a wooden bunk and a lidded slop bucket abuzz with flies. The iron bars in the one tiny window were set deep in the thick rock wall, and the cell door was of bars spaced six inches apart.

Freis was right; she wasn't going anywhere for the moment. She was determined to try breaking out, however, and would as soon as Ki showed up. Since he hadn't been on the road he should have been on with a doctor in tow, Jessie reasoned Ki could've been delayed and still be in town. That thought gave her comfort—until she realized a doctor might not've been available, in which case Ki would've returned via his short cut. Luckily she hadn't been searched or left handcuffed. Freis apparently assumed she was unarmed and defenseless. But a lot of good being able to spring her derringer did with nobody around close enough to draw it on.

Jessie idled away the evening. From her barred window, she could glance sidewards to the street where across from the jail some townsfolk were gathering, doubtlessly attracted by reports of her arrest. Growing noisier with questions and opinions, the group was continuing to expand when dusk had faded almost to dark. Jessie glimpsed a familiar wagon passing by. She recognized the weary figures of Duncan and Rachel and knew within minutes they would learn the grim news that supposedly explained Zack Biggs' death. Sorrow and anger weighed heavy on her heart.

Night encroached. Softened lamplight reflected from the street. No visitors came, no knocks on the front door, and neither lawman checked in. The throng out front was now blurred, but from that murky swarm and the adjacent saloons she could hear an increasing clamor of drunken shouts, harsh curses, and vicious laughter, all filtering in like rising portents.

Eventually the door opened and Deputy Bruno entered with a supper tray. "What a waste of pork chops," he muttered, shuffling across to put the tray on the desk. He scratched a match, and in its flame, his face took on a sinister pall. He bent to light the wick of a lamp. "Waste of prime female too, but can't be helped."

He was replacing the lamp's chimney when Duncan Biggs suddenly barged into the office. "Sir, you met me earlier tonight," Duncan yelled at the startled deputy, "when I transported here the remains of my sainted father and was apprised of his heinous demise!"

"Yeah, you're Zack's son, but—"

"We must confront evil to annihilate it," Duncan raged on, sweeping past and across to the cell, his eyes piercing with denunciation. "Repent, ye handmaiden of Lucifer! Repent before you are consigned to the eternal fires of perdition!"

Jessie was as nonplussed as Bruno. "I've nothing to repent!"

"Nothing to repent!" Duncan roared. "You have conspired to rob an honorable man and have slain him by diabolical torture. You have sinned, sinned sorely, and are an abomination unto our Lord!"

"I am not! You're wrong, Duncan," she asserted brittlely.

Turning, Duncan glowered at the deputy. "A Bible! A Bible shall be required to exorcise the demons from her soul. Be quick!"

"Yeah, yeah . . . I think one's around here somewhere."

Ignoring Bruno, Duncan knelt facing Jessie and unmistakably winked. "On your knees, witch. I shall suffer your confession."

Jessie dropped instantly, wailing, "Oh, I implore mercy!" Then keeping an eye on Bruno, who was dazedly ransacking desk drawers, she huddled close to Duncan at the bars.

"Sorry for my preachin'," Duncan whispered, "but I had to figure a way to get in and check what's against us here."

"The whole town," Jessie mouthed grimly. "Thanks."

"Town's nuts. I'll stake my life you didn't kill my father."

"I didn't. I'll explain, if I ever get the chance."

"You will. It appears to me we can pull the wagon round the side, snag a rope, and haul them bars clean outta your window."

Jessie gasped. "No, Duncan, please don't try."

"You think we'd leave you to swing? We were strangers and you saved us, and now we're friends and we're going to save you."

"Listen, staking your life, both your lives, is exactly what you're aiming to do. You attempt to break me from jail, and you'll be shot down or hounded as criminals. Duncan, do you want your niece to go to her grave branded an outlaw?"

"Nope, but she's as adamant as me. No use arguin'."

Nor could Jessie protest further, for Bruno had finished his rummaging and was turning toward them. Duncan, catching her signal, reared upright and launched another blast of fire and brimstone.

"You're damned!" he bellowed, wagging a finger. "I've heard only the blasphemous mewlings of an unrecalcitrant heathen!"

"Eh, Mr. Biggs, I can't find no Bible nowhere."

"Never mind, sir. The Bible directs us to offer succor and solace, but this shameless siren has cast her lot with Satan," Duncan declared, striding toward the door. "When she leaves this world, plant her face down so she'll know where she's heading." And with that, Duncan stormed like a cyclone out into the night.

"That gent almost flayed your hide, lady," Bruno snickered, relocking the door. "Well, you'll soon learn how right he is. Everyone's goaded up and lynch-talking, female be damned."

Jessie stood with both hands on her belt buckle. "I

don't suppose you and Marshal Freis will try to stop them, will you?"

"Why, sure," Bruno said, picking up the tray. "Of course, a mob is a powerful thing to buck, me and the marshal being two lone men against all those well-meaning friends and neighbors."

"Why, sure," Jessie echoed. "And who's buying them drinks?"

Bruno just shook his head and brought over the tray.

"It's like that, is it?"

"It's like that."

Thumbs hooked behind her buckle, Jessie leaned casually on the cell door. Bruno bent to slide the tray beneath it. Jessie's left hand abruptly thrust between the bars and fastened on Bruno's right shoulder at the tender nape of his neck. With her other hand, she snapped the derringer from the back of her buckle and jammed it against Bruno's left temple.

"Get up easy and open the cell," she ordered.

Bruno straightened, but then balked. "Hell, I will."

"You don't, you yell, or you fight—I'll blow your brains out."

"Dumb slut! Killing me won't get you free."

"I'm set to die anyway, right?" As Jessie spoke, her left hand darted to lift Bruno's holstered revolver. She backed off a pace. "Way I see it, if I'm going to die, we're going to die together."

From outside came sounds of saloons emptying and boots thumping on boardwalks. Soon the mob would reach a pitch and descend on the jail. Even sooner—at any moment, Jessie feared—Duncan and Rachel would try to rescue her, a foolishly gallant attempt she desperately wished to forestall. She feared they would be gunned

69

or lynched or be forced to become hunted fugitives for the rest of their days.

"Time's running out, Bruno." Jessie thumbed back the hammer of the deputy's .45, her hand trembling slightly. "For both of us."

Bruno looked at the quivering revolver and at Jessie's straining muscles and wild, tight eyes. Reluctantly he fumbled for the ring of keys in his pocket, selected a key, and inserted it. "Zack Biggs was loony, so was Thurlow," he growled, opening the door. "This latest one must be the looniest, though, 'cause I guess he slipped you that gun while you were praying."

"Me, get it from that pious idiot? Guess again." Jessie laughed contemptuously as she moved from the cell. "Turn around."

Bruno turned around. Reversing the revolver, Jessie whacked the butt down on his head. Bruno crumpled sideways on the floor.

Savoring a certain satisfaction, Jessie clipped the derringer back on her buckle and wedged the revolver into her belt. Swiftly she frisked the unconscious deputy, dragged him into the cell, locked the door, and pocketed the keys. Crossing to the rifle cabinet, she took the shotgun and ruined its breech by clubbing it against the desk, then she retrieved her own pistol and the saddlebags.

Then after gently easing the crossbar from the rear door, she slid out into the alley, which ran like an inky sewer behind the row of buildings. After a pause, she padded around the side to the shadows near the street and flattened against the wall. Peering, she saw the bloated mob was stirring expectantly, clogging much of the street with tentative advances, the men in front brandishing ropes. No sign of the marshal, but naturally there wouldn't be—Freis would be holed somewhere else, acting ignorant, leaving his deputy to defend the jail for a respectable period.

Cautiously Jessie retreated toward the rear, stopping a few yards from the alley to listen. The noisy crowd out front drowned whatever other sounds there might be. Risking it, she sprinted hunching around the corner in the direction of the livery, which she recalled having passed when entering the town—only to pull up short, almost tripping, as she tried to avoid colliding with a slow-moving wagon that seemingly had rolled from out of nowhere.

Rachel stared from the wagon. "What're you doing here?"

"What d'you think?" Jessie replied testily. "Go away."

"Sure. Climb into the bed."

Jessie shook her head. "My horse—"

"Is boarded at the stable, which's well lit and full of guys," Duncan cut in impatiently, craning around his niece. "Hells bells, get up and lay low, Jessie, and let us waltz you out of here."

Jessie hesitated, still reluctant to get them involved, yet prompted by the deadly threats emanating from the street.

"Hand her over, Bruno!"

"The floozie's guilty, we all know that!"

"Yeah! Nobody's gonna get hurt—'cept her!"

With a kind of grudging haste, Jessie climbed up, dived with the saddlebags through the rear canvas flap, and landed in a dense black welter of trunks, casks, bedding, and clothes. Promptly she burrowed deep under layers of blankets and felt the wagon sway and heard the wheels creak as Duncan jiggered his team forward.

They crept. Inching along made Jessie restive, even though she knew the alley must be narrow and cluttered and realized that Duncan was being properly careful and stealthy while he bypassed the street. Then suddenly the way grew impassable or Duncan lost his senses—Jessie couldn't tell which—but the wagon began lurching as it navigated a tight corner. They moved straight ahead, but now Jessie could hear the mob's shouts grow louder. Snaking out both pistols, she shifted to a more combative position, tensing anxiously while Duncan drove them directly into the street.

"Won't do no good to play possum, Bruno!"

"We know she's in there! Yeow! Rein them horses!"

"Make room!" Duncan's voice bellowed. "Make room!" In fits and starts, he plowed the wagon smack into the mob's midst, leaving a wake of men cursing, jostling, thumping the sideboards.

"Damnation, you nie run over my foot!"

"Whoa up! You ain't goin' nowhere; we'll see to that!"

The wagon jolted to a complete halt. Jessie cocked her pistols, eyeing the rear flap from beneath her cover and determined to blast the first who scrambled in and as many others as possible.

"Hey, I rec'lect you! Ain't you Zack's other boy?"

"Ain't fittin' for a son not to stay and watch."

"Is it fitting for an innocent lass to watch?" Jessie heard Duncan thunder, and she could envision him with a protective arm around Rachel. "We're all here for justice, gentlemen, but does that eliminate our compassion, our sense of chivalry?"

His rebuke had a chastening effect, Jessie noted, and calmer voices prevailed.

"Yeah, ain't decent her here."

"Go let her off and be quick about it."

Duncan tried to be quick about it. But the street was too jammed, and though some attempted to clear a path,

72

most of the pack remained intent on besieging the jail. A few of the more courageous banged fists on the front door, and when that failed to produce any results, cries arose to break in the door.

The wagon continued squeezing along at a crawl, seeming to take forever before Jessie finally could perceive a lessening of noise and crush. The wagon trundled faster, shuddering a little as if crossing a patch of washboard, then gently tilting one way and then the other. Reading the motions, Jessie surmised they were at the Sweetgum limits, where the street became the wagon road and wound through a lazy switchback curve flanked by trees.

She lowered her gunhammers and eased out from the blankets, not yet daring to breathe with relief. Sweat beading on her forehead and stinging her eyes, Jessie listened to the lynchers baying for blood and hammering rifle butts and truncheons against the jail's front door. Soon, surely, one of them would get the smarts to try the rear door, find it unbarred, enter and . . . Well, that mob could still turn into a posse. She wished Duncan would speed up.

Her wish was granted. It came without warning, just past the switchback beyond town. There was a whiplike crack and instantly the team bolted, yanking the wagon forward and pitching Jessie backward. She straightened, only to topple as the wagon slewed around the next, sharper bend. Again she struggled upright, but when the horses were lunging up the first of many slopes, she teetered, groped for support among the tumble of loose cargo, and flipped back against the tailgate.

"Dun–can!"

If Duncan heard, he ignored, hurrawing his team into renewed effort. For the next two miles Jessie reeled and sprawled and choked on dust, while the horses strained and sailed the wagon careening around corners, plunging into chuckholes, and catapulting over outcrops.

Finally, near the bottom of a hill, Duncan slowed the pell-mell charge to a walk and began to veer cautiously from the road. Jessie clambered to the tailgate, and lifting an edge of the canvas, she saw they were descending through dark masses of boulders and spruce to a creek bed. The wagon had a tendency to skid, but Duncan kept correcting by skillful control of his team, and he reined in by the stream without any great difficulty.

Jessie climbed out—stiff, sore, and exhausted.

"My horses need a rest," Duncan told her cheerily, while he and Rachel stepped to the creek. They knelt to drink, but as Jessie approached, Duncan glanced up and added, "Nobody'll spot us here. Hell, nobody's looking. We pulled it off clean."

Jessie eyed him skeptically. "As a getaway, this one left quite a deal to be desired," she grumped, kneeling to join them.

The trembling, heaving team had already sunk muzzles gratefully to the water and nearby grass. Jessie drank from the creek. The moon, emerging from behind banked clouds, illuminated the surrounding forest and the road—where despite Duncan's assurances, she realized, a posse might ride.

Duncan and Rachel's help may kill them, Jessie reflected, yet it may have kept them alive emotionally. Alone in a strange land and bereft by tragedy, they may have felt impelled to trust the one person they knew even slightly—other than Ki—unaware that by their act of faith, they were strengthening their own resolve, confirming belief in themselves.

Those values could use some bolstering, so when they

settled, Jessie said, "I know you're plagued with many questions you want answered, but I'd like to ask a couple first. Duncan, you told the deputy that you'd brought your father into town. How'd that come about?"

"Well, me'n Rachel followed our map and found the cabin and my father in a terrible state. Didn't know what'd occurred, except it wasn't natural, so we took him to Sweetgum for burial and the law."

"Did you happen to see Ki at the cabin or in town?"

Rachel shook her head. "Not at all. But I wish you to know I believe same's Uncle Dunc, Jessie, that you didn't torture him to death. I don't care what the marshal claims."

"Thanks, Rachel, for your vote of confidence. I promised your uncle I'd explain if given the chance. Now's the chance." With that, Jessie described the events since leaving the ferry landing and reported what she knew of Zack Biggs' sad end.

"There's no doubt in my mind that Zack was killed by Marshal Freis and Deputy Bruno," Jessie concluded, "in their attempts to make him tell where his cache of beaver skins is hidden."

Duncan frowned. "I wonder if they got him to spill."

Jessie shook her head. "Zack as good as told me he hadn't. He was raving just before he died, though, something about the secret being in Thurlow's brain, and something else about a silver skull. It made no sense. Zack got pretty delirious, I'm afraid."

"Sure, it makes some sense," Rachel said eagerly. "You remember, Uncle Dunc, how my dad and you were working in the oil fields, and he fell off some tower? And how some doctor sawed a hole in Dad's head, and he had a silver plate there afterward?"

"True, true. The company medico relieved the pressure on Thurlow's brain. The medico fitted a silver dollar into the hole, God's truth, and sewed up his scalp good as new. Thurlow joked that he'd never be broke." Duncan chuckled nostalgically, then grew somber. "Buck up, Rachel, I fear your pappy must be dead, too."

Rachel's chin began to quiver as she fought back tears. "I . . . I know, Uncle Dunc. Soon's everyone in town started telling us about Dad being missing all winter, I knew, I knew in my heart. Dad would never be gone that long or quit writing us, unless . . ."

"There, there, we still got each other. I'll be good to you, you'll see." Sighing heavily, he glanced at Jessie and his eyes hardened with bitterness. "Them outlaw lawdogs must've bagged Thurlow, I bet, and for the same reason, to get their bloody mitts on that fortune in pelts. Well, laugh's on them; it's lost forever. Whatever secret my paw was rambling about before he died, he and my brother took it with them to their graves."

"Y'know what else, Uncle Dunc? I think the marshal or the deputy was the ambusher who cut our ferry loose. They didn't want us coming here to find the stash."

"That's reasonable," Duncan allowed.

"Possibly, but it hasn't much bearing on matters now," Jessie hedged. "What's more important is that your own lives are in constant danger. Assume for sake of argument that you get away with helping me escape, you're still marked for the cemetery by Freis and Bruno, who'll stoop to anything to stop you or force you into disclosing the cache's location."

"But we don't know the location," Rachel objected.

"You know, and I know, but they don't know you don't know."

Duncan's eyes twinkled with malicious amusement. "Just let them try. For that account, just let them try to harm you, Jessie. Say, you're kinda in a pickle, too. What're your plans?"

"I'm in bit of a quandary," Jessie admitted. "I could go to Emerald Timber Company—I can anytime—but what I really think I should do is locate Ki. We've missed connecting since he left your cabin, and I feel responsible because I'm the one who said I'd be waiting when he returned from town with a doctor for Zack."

"Of course, that's who it is!" Duncan declared abruptly, snapping his fingers. "Calm your fears; he's at Emerald."

"How on earth would you know a thing like that?"

"The marshal, indirectly. He introduced me around while he bragged of your arrest, and in one saloon we met up with his deputy, who was feeding whiskey to an Emerald logging man already drunker'n a boiled owl. While we were chatting, the logger kept droning and the deputy kept shushing him and pouring drinks. But the gist of it was that he'd been sent to town to get the sawbones to visit a place on the slim chance the big Chink—as he called him—they were holding was telling true. Y'see? It all fits—somehow."

Jessie nodded thoughtfully. "Did the logger mention what they would do to the man if his story was untrue?"

Duncan drew a finger across his throat.

"Well, Ki's story won't be true. Zack and I aren't there," Jessie said agitatedly. "That means he's in trouble because whatever reason Emerald has for holding him can't be a nice one."

"We'd better get there, then. I'll cinch the horses."

"Hurry! My nerves aren't calming, not at all!"

Chapter 8

Ki was in trouble, all right. He was confronting death.

Trapped in the confining shed, he faced the burly loggers crowding the doorway and knew that anything he might try to tell them would be laughed off. They'd proven his story false, and Gerry Shaw, his desire for vengeance white-hot, was not to be denied his chance.

Swiftly two of the vigilantes slid past Gerry, one man carrying a strip of gunny sack, the other a coil of rope. In desperation, Ki angled himself to put the man with the rope between him and Gerry's pointed revolver and speared his stiffened hand into the man's abdomen. Gagging, the man sagged, reeling and falling back against Gerry. The other men prepared to gang up on Ki.

Ki launched himself at the next closest logger, aware that he was doomed if he failed to fight his way out of the shed. Again he stabbed with his right hand, this time using the callused edge of the palm like a shearing cleaver. With his left he struck at another man in a *nakadata-ippon-ken,* or middle-knuckle punch to the throat.

The results were agonized gruntings and scuffled stumblings, yet even as Ki pivoted to press his attack,

Shaw plunged in from behind, lashing with his revolver. Seeing the looming rush, Ki tried to duck and twist away, but he lacked sufficient space to elude the blow entirely. Gerry slashed his gun at Ki's head with stunning force, and unfortunately for Ki, he clubbed the same point where the peavy had injured him before. Already suffering the effects of a concussion there, Ki felt himself sinking to the floor, almost blacking out.

The other men swarmed over him before he could recover. His arms were jerked behind his back, his wrists and then his ankles bound securely with logging rope. The strip of gunny sack was stuffed in his mouth to prevent an outcry that would rouse the camp and bring Hans Aubrecht. Hauled roughly to his feet, he was positioned then beneath the shed's main rafter. Ki swayed, woozy and powerless in the grip of the men who held his trussed arms.

The long coil of rope was retrieved by the man who'd brought it, and Ki felt his throat constrict as he saw the noose tied at one end. The man tossed the rope over the rafter. Gerry, after jabbing his revolver in his belt, caught the noose and fit it over Ki's head. Then he drew the rope snug around, his every movement expressing his unquenchable rage.

Obeying Gerry's gesture, the other loggers took grips on the rope's end, drawing in the slack until the pressure threatened to choke Ki. Gerry stepped back, his face satanic in the flickering lantern light. He stood close to realizing his revenge. When he signaled his accomplices, they would wrench Ki as high as the rafter. If his neck were not snapped by the jerk, Ki would die slowly, strangling.

His back to the shed door, Ki kept his gaze riveted

on Gerry, waiting for him to give the signal.

"If you meet up with my brother, tell him some more Bar-Emmers will be along pronto if they try what you did," Gerry said, gloating. Then he addressed the men. "Okay, hang him."

"Hang Ki, and you'll hang for murder!"

The voice was sharp yet breathless. Ki heard the abrasive scrape of boots on packed earth and saw Gerry's eyes bulging and his face paling. Ki whirled about, twisting the rope. And grinned.

Jessie was in the vanguard; Duncan and Rachel followed. At her side ran Margot Gideon, who then thrusted through the crestfallen men who'd let go of the rope. She had shouted, and as she furiously worked the noose off Ki's neck, it was her flinty voice that ordered, "Cut his ropes; cut them off this instant!"

No longer the avenging hero, Gerry snatched a knife from his pocket. "We was only payin' him his dues for killing Leroy."

"The less you say about trying to string up Ki the better," Margot snapped. "The lady by the door happens to be Miss Starbuck."

"The–the owner?" Gerry gaped at Jessie, then hastily began sawing through the ropes binding Ki's wrists. "I– I reckon then it was all true," he said, sounding as if a bone were caught in his throat. He stooped and sliced the ropes around Ki's ankles. He then straightened up. "I . . . I'm sorry. Lordy, am I sorry!"

Free of his ropes, Ki flashed Jessie a smile of relief and reassurance. Then he regarded Gerry sternly. "Not as sorry as I'd have been if they hadn't stopped you. I'll overlook it because I know you were half-crazy over your brother's death, but that's the limit."

"N—no, er, yes, sir. W—won't be no more trouble, I promise." Gerry faltered, his chagrined abettors chorusing agreement.

"Better not be or you'll be lots sorrier," Jessie warned. "If Ki's willing to forgive, so be it, but I'm not going to forget."

"And I may not be ready to do so either," Margot threatened darkly. "But I've a hunch your real apologies are coming when you try to explain to Hans Aubrecht what happened to his prisoner. Now, get!"

The penitent loggers left the shed, while Jessie and the Biggses joined Margot with Ki. "Thanks, all of you," Ki said with gratitude. "I was a goner, but I'm okay now. Jessie, let's talk."

Jessie nodded. "We definitely should."

"Let's go to my office," Margot suggested and led the way outside.

En route to Margot's bungalow, Ki was told of how Jessie had raced to the Emerald with Duncan and Rachel, had awakened Margot, and headed for the shed. They spotted its door ajar and the scene inside.

Further recounting waited until Margot ushered them into her combination front parlor and office. The room's decor reflected both uses: chintz curtains and filing cabinets, a brocade sofa and chair set, and a desk fashioned from a shellacked slab of tree trunk with stumps for legs. From a cabinet Margot removed a bottle of whiskey, her hand trembling slightly as she poured some in each of five glasses and passed them around.

"I think a nip would do us all some good," she said. After they each had a sip, she continued, "Managing Emerald has been hard, especially since Eliot died, but that's no excuse. Responsibility for Ki's horrid treatment falls on my shoulders. Now that you're here, Miss Starbuck, I suppose you'll want to take over from me."

"Please, call me Jessie. And no, I want you to stay."

Margot's gaze met Jessie's eyes. "Are you positive?"

"Positive. Hindsight is perfect. Under the circumstances you can't be faulted. Besides, I'm hardly in a position to crow," Jessie added wryly and related her own brush with lynchers, her status as a fugitive, and how Marshal Freis was to blame.

"Cold-blooded scoundrel!" Margot flared and explained about Freis also being the lawyer for the Bar M and the beef syndicate. "This confirms my feeling that the Bar M rider Ki saw was sent by Freis and that Liam McManus didn't have a hand in killing my rigger."

Duncan gave a snort. "Pardon my intrudin', ma'am, but thems who get cozy with mad dogs generally wind up with rabies."

"You've got a point there," Ki said with a chuckle, as he stood inspecting a large-scale contour map on the wall. "Whether McManus sent the rider or not, his lawsuits show he's after Emerald. I'm curious why. If I read this map right, he couldn't run his cattle up in these timber sections, doesn't need more water, and already has the best grazing land around."

"He wants to shut us down, Ki, not take us over," Margot replied. "Too many ranchers and farmers have been victims, I'm afraid, of loggers spoiling watersheds by clearing hillsides above ranch lands. It's a fallacy that a forest needs to be laid bare in order to make lumber, but McManus refuses to believe we won't do that and refuses to work with us. He is obstinately convinced by his own blather that we'll wipe him out with floods and erosions."

"Well, there's the motive," Rachel declared.

"For his injunctions," Jessie replied, pacing the room.

"I sense there's more to it, motives that tie to Freis. Follow my thinking: According to my attorneys, McManus was duped by the syndicate; Grand Americana sold land it didn't own, just had a long-term lease for— same as we've got here. Grand Americana has an unsavory reputation. It is one knot in a tangled web of blind trusts and interlocking companies, but it's never before been caught in a fraud. I suspect that's because some overly greedy small fry actually conned McManus. But once stuck with the swindle, the syndicate had to close ranks to keep it from being discovered. What do you think, Ki, am I making any sense?"

Ki nodded thoughtfully. "Plenty. McManus's legal actions threaten to expose all of the syndicate's crooked house of cards. Freis means to prevent this by forcing Emerald to fold first. He'll kill to do it, and he'll blame it all on the Bar M if there're repercussions. If he sparks a cattle-timber war, even better; the victor won't be interested in pursuing a dead issue in court."

"Will you let it get that bad? I mean, there're rumors that Starbuck, well, is too huge and remote to bother with a small and seemingly stillborn subsidiary. I'm sure the yarns are being spread by those Freis calls deputies, but you know how jacks talk. Always some who'll grumble about bosses." Margot paused, a pleading expression in her eyes. "Will Starbuck support us?"

"Yes, fully. To do otherwise would be unthinkable. Freis is an evil man, too evil to be allowed to win."

"Then, Jessie, you've got a camp of loyal fighters. They're scrappy and tough, as I think Ki can testify to after today."

They laughed good-naturedly at that; then Jessie grew serious again. "But I don't want it to get to be a war. I want to stop it before it starts because Emerald and Bar

M both will wind up dead losers, and only Freis and the syndicate will be winners."

Ki nodded emphatically. "I think some investigating is in order. Tomorrow morning I'll scout around that blasted spar for clues and, if you'll help, Margot, maybe we can trace the killer."

"I'll be happy to, Ki. Dear me, tomorrow morning is today, and I've yet to arrange accommodations for you and Jessie."

"Margot," Jessie said regretfully, "I'm a jailbreaker, and staying here could bring unnecessary dangers. It won't take long for Freis to discover I'm truly who I told him I was and to deduce I would most likely hole up on Starbuck property. Freis might well get the idea of using me as an excuse to raid Emerald with a big posse."

"I'll rouse the men and we'll fight—"

"Exactly what I want to avoid. We'll play rough and for keeps, but I want to use brain power more than gunpowder. Lend me a bedroll and a good horse, and I'll drift upland. If Freis should hit, don't do anything. Just be cooperative and ignorant."

The others' expressions made it clear they understood her position and knew she was leaving for Emerald's sake. Nonetheless, Rachel protested, "Camping out isn't ladylike, and you still could be tracked. Hide at our cabin, Jessie, please. Who'd ever dream to look for you with us?"

"Freis will, if he suspects you helped me escape."

"I keep telling you, he won't," Duncan insisted. "That's one reason I drove into the mob, that and the garbage pile blocking the alley. Nobody'd believe we'd try such a dumb, blatant getaway—us, the kin of the man you murdered. But I happen to believe that Freis has us marked for killing. So you'll not only be a welcome guest, but a blessed boon in case of trouble."

"I'm tempted, but..."

"And another thing, just to show you where we stand. Me and Rachel got kinda discouraged and planned to tuck tail back to Indiana. But after listening to all your pluck, I for one have changed my mind. I'd like to see this thing out, to avenge my family, and to set root here."

"Count me in, too, Uncle Dunc," Rachel interjected. "I'm not going to let a couple of bent badges rob us of our dream."

Duncan drew his body up to its full height. "That's the spirit, gal. Tomorrow you'n me will go to Sweetgum and see about inheritin' your grandpaw's place, and maybe about locatin' our own homestead, too. We'll get along fine without that beaver cache—with the help of friends like ours."

"Very well, you've talked me into it," Jessie said, proud to accept the offer of such brave souls. "Margot, I'll still need the horse and bedroll, but first..."

"Yes?"

"How about another drop of whiskey and a bite to eat?"

Chapter 9

Ki slept on the office sofa.

He'd have preferred not to. But by the time Jessie saddled a strawberry mare and left with the Biggses, it was too late to disturb the bunkhouse crew—or so Margot insisted, despite the seeming impropriety of Ki's staying with her. Their conduct was above reproach, not that any jack would dare insinuate otherwise; their boss was sacrosanct. Still, Ki would've preferred to sleep elsewhere, finding the sofa too soft and spongy for his comfort.

After too few hours rest, Ki and Margot headed for breakfast. At benched tables under a vapor of steam and tobacco smoke, eighteen jacks were already wolfing flapjacks and bacon. All were in flannel shirts and cord pants, and most had on laced hobnail boots. A third were in muddy boots, and it took Ki a moment to realize these must be the men detailed to dam the river. Though Margot also was dressed in logger's garb, she wore high-heeled riding boots. There were other outstanding differences to her appearance, Ki noticed with pleasure, which set her further apart from her crew.

"Boys, listen up," she announced. "In spite of what

some of you pulled, Miss Starbuck is not quitting and has pledged to stick and fight. Neither she nor I is asking any of you to risk his neck. It wasn't part of your job when you hired on, so you can keep out and nobody'll think any less of you for it."

Nobody responded at once. Then a towheaded jack stood and hunched forward. "Ain't mucha fight Bjorn can't handle, yah-sure."

Hans Aubrecht hooted, "Maybe you hope to whip Bar M alone if you drink enough booze, you knucklehead." Laughter erupted. Then Hans arose, his jaw set belligerently. "I speak for us all, Boss. Tell us when and where, and we'll fight."

A burst of applause confirmed unanimous support. Margot and Ki settled down to breakfast.

Soon they left camp, Ki on his roan and Margot on a pinto, and took the trail that Ki and the loggers had walked the previous day. The sun lifted over the crags, dispelling the purple shadows of the forest as they rode along, and it was spilling its golden shower into the clearing when they arrived and dismounted.

Together they began a methodical search, concentrating on the spar's splintered base and the thicket where Ki first had spied the rider. They failed to find what Ki suspected they might—bits of powder cartridges, snaking wires, or a detonator. Instead, they located tiny burn lines, some confetti of waxed paper, and twisted shards of a tin can.

The charge must have been wrapped in waxed paper and ignited by a lit fuse. Ki was able to piece together enough of the tin can to determine it had been a container of black powder used in loading choke-bore shotgun shells, not used for blasting trees down. It had worked—

most anything would've worked—but it indicated the rider had been a crude amateur when it came to operating explosive devices.

Satisfied, Ki led Margot out to the spot where the rider had wheeled his Bar M horse and fled. Broken branches told how the rider had sent his horse crashing headlong through a clump of ailanthus. Ki studied the ground where imprints retained by disturbed leaf mold showed how the horse had stood, been mounted, and spurred to galloping. After familiarizing himself with the peculiarities of the horse's shod hooves, Ki briefly scouted the ailanthus clump and returned to Margot.

"Okay, now we follow that path."

"Could be a hard chore in this timber," she cautioned, as they started back to the clearing for their horses. But Ki had stalked Indians whose instincts made them as cunning and difficult to trap as beasts and whose brains made them much more dangerous. Trailing the rider might be difficult, yes, but not impossible.

From the far side of the clump, the track plunged through forest in a southwesterly direction. For a time Ki was able to read the signs without dismounting, for there was scarcely any underbrush. The woods were a mature stand of huge conifers, uniformly sized and widely spaced, rising straight and branchless to great heights before their tops unfurled.

Soon they crossed a wagon road, which Margot explained was the drive from the main road to the camp. Ki could hear birds chattering from bowers along the shoulders, but once back under the high canopy of trees, there was silence. It made the forest seem impermeable and eternal and made Ki feel ephemeral and insignificant. Eventually the imposing stand softened into a landscape of average groves, stone ledges, and rough brakes, which in turn ended at the steep banks of a brutal, white-rapids river.

"The Vicar, the river we want to dam and the center of our legal dispute," Margot said. "He can't have forded it here."

"Not lest his horse sprouted wings," Ki replied, gazing at the mountain torrent down in a gorge matted with pine and scrub. Checking about, he spotted indentations left by the horse and motioned to Margot to fall in as he followed the path downstream.

The hoofprints finally cut riverward where the banks dipped in a rounded slope. Less compressed here, the Vicar appeared to be slightly wider and calmer, yet its foaming, swirling rush was still sufficient to cause any person to approach it with apprehension and great care.

"Better. Not by much," Ki judged, "but the rider crossed here. I'll admit, the Vicar will serve as an excellent log chute."

She laughed. "When our dam's finished, it'll ebb to no more than a trickle between mud puddles. Well, let's get this over with."

Horses prancing, shying, they kept firm rein and kneed forward, forcing their reluctant mounts to wade in up to the hocks in icy water. Urged on, the horses struggled across—hooves fighting the slippery, sharp rocks; legs resisting the churning current. Sliding, almost slipping, they pawed up the other bank and, before proceeding, stood huffing and shivering for a recuperative moment.

During that pause, Ki glanced at the Vicar and recalled what Jessie had said was the reason for damming it. A lake would form behind the dam, into which logs would be rolled and stored. When enough water and logs were built up, the dam would be opened and the logs sluiced down to the Rogue, and thence to the railroad and mills at Grants Pass. It would be an ideal arrangement, assuming Emerald could win the legal right to dam.

From the river, the way grew more difficult to follow since growth flourished, interspersed with hard rock. Increasingly Ki had to dismount and scrutinize the terrain ... ferreting the occasional hoofprint, the white scratch of iron shoe against stone, the cracked twig still pithy green inside ... deciphering the trail slowly and painstakingly yet with grim satisfaction.

Once he discovered where the rider had stopped, his mount having cropped leaves from a bush, its stripped branches sticky with congealing sap. And it was then that Margot pointed at an old, dead spruce.

"That tree is on Bar M's range," she said.

"Well, we're shagging a Bar M horse." Ki moved on, adding, "At the risk of upsetting your good opinion of Liam McManus, I've got an inkling this trail is liable to wind up on his doorstep."

He spoke the words lightly, but there was a tone that brought a sharp glance from Margot. "Why, you sound just like Eliot when he'd tease me about some notion of mine."

"Sorry. Didn't mean to sport him or hurt you."

"Oh, no, tweaked a nerve, is all. Last time he joshed me, I felt wrong about him going alone to town. We'd been expecting retaliation after he and a couple of the crew got the better of three Bar M hands in a bar. Next day Bjorn found him savagely beaten and comatose. Sent for Doc Harn. No luck. Three days unconscious." Margot slumped in her saddle. "We buried Eliot in back of the bungalow."

"And the Bar M?"

"We knew some of them did it, but what could we

91

prove? McManus denied everything. He visited to offer condolences, and in his own manner, he acted sincere. I spit in his eye, but I remember even then wondering if he knew much about it." Her shoulders stiffened and her back straightened, but her voice began a muttering to herself, and Ki saw a wildness sear her eyes. "Now I wonder more if Freis and his thugs didn't get my husband, like they got Zack and Thurlow, and probably Leroy. Clubbed him to death, that's what they did to my Eliot." She shot a glance at Ki and a flush tinged her cheeks. "Forget it."

They pressed onward. Meadows and sloping grasslands were becoming more prevalent, but so were tangled depressions of hickory, thistle, and wild rose, and brush-cluttered stretches of aspen, birch, and white oak. By now Ki had deduced a pattern, a habit of shifting course to suit the terrain, rather than altering erratically to throw off any pursuers. The balance of the hunt was ridden at as swift a pace as prudent tracking would allow, and before long they reached the lip of a ridge where, reining up, they saw Ki's prophecy was correct.

Ki and Margot overlooked a group of barns, corrals, and other buildings nestled in a grassy hollow between two hills. Smoke curled from a cookhouse flue, a blacksmith's hammer clanged on an anvil, and men went about their tasks or watched horses being broken in. Fastened atop the main gate to the grounds was a Conestoga wheel, its hub removed and its spokes made into the logo of the Bar M Ranch.

Ki sat quietly surveying the yard, focusing on each man to see if he could identify one in particular. The distance was too far to be certain, and they all appeared to be lacking peculiarities, such as flamboyantly squashed red noses.

Mulling over the situation, Ki remarked, "To beat 'em, get to know 'em. About now it wouldn't hurt to plant a fox in McManus' chicken coop."

"You? Spy on them?" Incredulity crossed Margot's face. "Be serious! They'll know you and'll beat you senseless."

"Only Emerald and the Biggses have seen me personally. That drunken sot you sent for the doctor last night sure talked about me, so better have your crew gossip that I was lynched. Orientals aren't uncommon, and you know how it goes—can't tell us apart, we all look alike." Ki flashed her a wry grin. "A risk, granted, but there's a greater chance they simply won't want to hire me on. Have you a gun?"

Reluctantly Margot dug into her saddle pouch and handed across a coiled shell belt with a holstered S&W .44 American. Ki buckled the rig on, thankful for his slim waist, telling her, "I'll try to pass word back to you. If your jacks see me somewhere, they're to act like I'm a stranger. They're not to give any recognition, whatever is done or said, whatever may be happening."

"Don't gamble your life. Promise me you won't."

She remained leaning toward him, her face poised so close that—a notion sparked in Ki, which he promptly squelched. For an instant it had seemed to him almost as though she were offering her mouth to him, but that was ridiculous.

"Margot, life is a gamble. I can't promise any outcome."

She kissed him then. It wasn't a peck; it wasn't a smooch; it was the sweet compress of her lips against his. "Good-bye," she said hastily, and without hesitation she wheeled her pinto and spurred back through the brush.

Ki lingered, listening to the receding drum of hoofbeats. At last he turned and heeled his roan into a lope along the ridge, skirting behind the shorter of the hills and looping around to approach the Bar M from the front. Once past the entrance gates, he trotted up a poplar-lined drive to the main yard. There he halted prominently in the open and, in accordance with ranch etiquette, stayed mounted until he was acknowledged. While he waited, he made another appraisal of the men who were about, again failing to tag any as the man he sought.

Soon a big, grizzled puncher wearing a Stetson and a full set of whiskers sauntered over from the corral. "I'm Sam Ledbetter, the ramrod here. Step down and cool your saddle."

"Ulysses Fong," Ki replied as he dismounted. "Any chance of hiring on this spread?"

"P'raps. I'm short-handed, but it ain't up to me. Decidin' on jobs is all done by our boss, Liam McManus," Ledbetter explained and tugged at his beard. "Fong, eh? Reckon you must be fresh green in these parts, to be askin' at the Bar M."

"Looks like a swell outfit to me. What's the hook?"

Ledbetter dodged answering and began traipsing off. "Go on 'cross to the wranglers' c'ral and see Mr. McManus. Whether he takes you or not, drop by the cookshack and strap on a feedbag."

Ki called his thanks, feeling his curiosity piqued. He'd been anticipating the Bar M to be filled with rogues, but his initial impression of Ledbetter was that he was a competent, honorable foreman. Hitching his roan at a nearby rack, he went to the corral. Strung along its pole fence, hurrawing cowboys were watching a wrangler tame a maverick. The exhibition was fairly exciting, but Ki concentrated on the spectators as he circled the fence.

There was no mistaking which was Liam McManus.

94

Fiftyish, he was large, fleshy, though none of it was fat, and handsome in his bullish way. He wore a brown suit and string tie, and his boots were Spanish-tooled. There was Irish blood evident in his face and ruddy hair.

"Mister McManus? I'm Ulysses Fong."

Turning from the horse show, McManus irritably regarded Ki. "Saints, a coolie in cowpoke duds. What is it you want, boy?"

Ki stiffened. He realized the taunt was not meant in earnest. Still, he resented the crack, and took a deep breath before responding.

"Your foreman told me to see you about a job."

"Sorry, we already have a cook. A good one."

"I'm not a cook. I'm not a housekeeper, either."

"You're also not what I'm needing. Fact is, I'm only after salty buckaroos who can deal out miseries." He shifted back to view the show, but when he grew aware that Ki wasn't moving, he confronted Ki again with a mixture of disdain and exasperation. "Are you deaf? Anyone who works for me draws himself a stake in a war. I'm renting guns as much or more as cow savvy."

Ki looked unimpressed. "How much do you pay?"

"About thirty."

"Sheepherders earn more'n that."

"Consider yourself good, do you?"

"I've been in a fight once or twice. Even been known to shoot off my pistol three times in a row, and that's a fact."

"Wonderful," McManus said scornfully.

"Mainly, though," Ki continued, "I'm a powderman."

"We've got a blaster. A good one."

"Not as good as me, I bet," Ki said with smug confidence. "Why don't you bring him here and we'll talk it over? You'll see."

95

McManus paused, a malicious gleam seeping into his green eyes. Ki's pulse quickened as McManus rose to the bait. "Right, Fong, why not?" he agreed smoothly and then stepped to the closest puncher, ordering, "Get the Canuck over here, on the double."

Ki waited expectantly, eager to talk over more than just a job and to talk with more than just his mouth. It was evident the French-Canadian was part of the Bar M's crew, which spoiled Margot's opinions about McManus and Jessie's theories about Freis. A pity, but the important fact was that the Canuck was the ranch's blaster who, contrary to McManus' boast, had been a poor one when he'd blasted the tree and killed the rigger. Having snared the Canuck, Ki was impatient to reel in his catch.

When the puncher returned, however, the man with him did not resemble the rider Ki had glimpsed. His face sported a Gallic nose, and he was taller, broader, and thicker than the rider, and a good fifty pounds heavier, too. It was hard to guess his age. But his occupation was obvious, for his shirt was off, and from his black hair to his waist, he was grimy with sweat and soot. He was the blacksmith.

The smith plodded toward the corral, swinging the wooden shank off some wagon harness. Reaching McManus, he stopped and planted his feet wide. "I been repairing the harness like you say. You wan' to see or you wan' something else?"

McManus laughed jovially. "I want you to hear this brave bucko here. He's of a mind to take your job, Henri, isn't that funny?"

Henri stood hunched forward as though the sky were too low for him, letting the idea percolate through. Then he decided to laugh, too, his chortle rumbling from the depths of his massive chest. "Eh, a fine joke." He ceased laughing and his face became truculent. He lifted the shank overhead as if it were some sort of battle standard and said, "You know I be the Canuck?"

"Not till now," Ki replied, wishing he still didn't.

"You don't ever hear of Henri the Canuck? Where you come from you never hear of Henri the Canuck? You fun with me more, I got a good notion to break your neck with this stick."

Ki kept his mouth shut. He was neatly mousetrapped and increasingly encircled as hands came flocking. Glumly, Ki realized that he'd been fed his own bait and a touch of blarney. And Margot had scoffed at McManus' being a sly dog.

"You think I cannot?" Henri roared, apparently enraged by Ki's not responding. He drew himself back in a manner designed to make Ki shrink before his tremendous size. He started forward, evidently expecting Ki to retreat.

Instead, Ki shifted his feet, took a half step forward, and struck Henri with a right-left combo to the chest, thinking as he punched that he mustn't use his martial arts training. To do so would've ended this fight in short shrift and perhaps ended Henri permanently. But his seemingly strange and unique methods would have created a furor, the attention likely backfiring against him and his mission. He'd have to beat Henri at his own game, the cruder yet accepted technique of the common brawling match.

Henri rook Ki's jolting blows, grunting twice, and merely seeming to absorb the force of them. The shaft never wavered until Henri swung it down with a force that would have cleaved Ki's skull, if Ki hadn't been ready and danced aside.

Missing threw Henri off balance. He was turned partly

away, his belly unprotected, and Ki hit him again. It was perfectly timed, a flurry of jabs to solar plexus and gut, and another right to the heart. But Henri remained on his feet. He absorbed punishment, and Ki began wondering if anything short of a sledgehammer would put the Canuck down and out.

Henri began to turn, tripped, lost his footing, and abruptly sat down. Before Ki could attack, he twisted over on hands and knees, crouching like a sprinter.

"So. You wan' figh' with Henri the Canuck. Henri rather figh' than eat frogs and drink wine."

He tossed the shaft aside and charged with his arms wide open. Instead of meeting Henri directly, Ki side-stepped at the last instant, figuring Henri would go past him. The Canuck was quicker than any man would expect. He turned and forced Ki back. Retreating, Ki delivered swift, short-range knucklers. There was no trick to hitting the big man, but it seemed futile, for Henri ignored the blows and kept advancing.

The corral fence gouged Ki's back, one post catching his heel. He tried to get his balance. Henri stormed in atop him. They caromed, fell, and rolled in the dust. Henri let his momentum carry him on and lurched upright, dragging Ki along by the hair. Ki butted him hard, breaking free. Henri swung his fist in a narrow arc, bending his arm at the final instant. The fist deliberately missed its mark and his elbow struck with the stunning power of a bludgeon.

Ki felt the breath go out of him and staggered, smashing into the fence again. He fell, landing on his back. A wild yell erupted from Henri, savage confidence lighting his face. Instinctively, Ki doubled both legs with knees beneath his chin as Henri came charging in. At the last instant, Henri comprehended and tried to stop, but he

98

was too late. Ki's legs uncoiled and snapped, his callused heels stabbing Henri in the pit of his stomach. The Canuck reeled, gasping and groaning, and crashed to the ground.

The crew had cheered enthusiastically when Ki hit the dirt, but now that their man was down, their shouts grew lusty with calls to get up. Henri rolled sideways, scrambling to regain his feet in that waiting stance of his. Ki straightened quickly, knowing Henri wouldn't stay crouched for long and thinking the fight must be fought differently. Body blows didn't hurt Henri, but those were the only shots open to a shorter man badly outweighed and with a shorter reach. Scrutinizing Henri, Ki was suddenly aware of that pristine nose—and the lack of scars or any real damage to his features. Nobody ever had gotten to Henri's face.

Ki set himself, eyes sweeping the hungry crowd and glimpsing McManus leaning indolently against the fence. Again Henri surged and again Ki sprang aside. But this time Ki jumped as well, angling a straight-arm punch higher, his fist crunching into Henri's cheek. The recoil jarred Ki and sent pain stabbing through his arm, but when Henri pivoted, Ki forgot the pain, seeing the flesh on Henri's cheek laid open in a long crimson furrow. Blood was dripping down his face and he stood, tasting it, disbelieving.

Another charge and a drilling sock to Henri's left eye that gashed a cut in the brow. Henri, bellowing, reacted with instinctual swiftness, and before Ki could evade the groping arms, Henri had him clamped in a bear hug.

Ki felt his breath squeezed from his chest, pain sharp in his rib cage. Only his right arm was free of Henri's tightening vice, and it had no arc of motion and little strength. But a fury of desperation put force into the short pummeling jabs he landed behind Henri's ear. For a fraction of a second Henri's grip relaxed. Frantically Ki wrenched away, sliding down through the band of arms, and skipped nimbly free.

Half blinded by blood, Henri lumbered, pawing. This was no time to chance being trapped by those arms again. Ki leaped. The thrust of his own lunge, combined with Henri's rush, coalesced into a blow that hit Henri's chin with a jolting shock. Henri stumbled backward, and it was then, that instant, Ki realized he had a glass jaw. A giant, a bull of strength, but with a jaw that betrayed. Immediately Ki dived, pressing his advantage.

Henri had his hands part way up, looking at Ki with blurred, half comprehending eyes. If he saw the strike coming, he made no counter to fend it off. Ki's left fist to the chin rocked Henri back on his heels. Ki's blow launched Henri spinning and then collapsing flat on his face. He lay unmoving for a few seconds, before slowly struggling to his knees.

Ki headed for him. He knew the rules or the lack of them, knew that having downed his man, he should kick and stomp him to a pulp. A moment ago, the crew had been yelling for Henri to maul him. Now it was Henri who was vulnerable, and the whole sweating batch of them tensed for Ki to claim his right.

Henri watched Ki, scrunching guardedly against an attack. Instead, Ki extended his hand, and when Henri flinched from accepting it, he grabbed Henri and forcibly helped him upright. He grinned genially. "You're a great fighter and smithy, Henri the Canuck."

Henri tottered, suspicious. "Eh?"

"You fooled me plenty. You were too quick for me. I can't whip a good fighter like you, Henri, or best a good blacksmith like you, either. You stay the smith, and I'll find another job to work."

"Tha' righ'?" Henri looked confused, having expected trouble and unprepared for praise. He got more as the crew clustered about, congratulating both men for a rousing match. Henri blinked dirt from his eyes and joined in chuckling. "I been never licked. I am Henri the Canuck, the blacksmith."

Ki pulled away and went to McManus.

Chapter 10

Ki was made to earn his wages sooner than expected.

During the short time before lunch, Ledbetter showed Ki where to bunk and some of the layout. Then the iron triangle by the cookhouse clanged, and everyone assembed for chow. The hands ate voraciously, bantering and griping and discussing the fight, including Ki in their camaraderie as one of their own.

When second helpings were being scooped, the door opened and McManus entered. Behind him trooped a man who, the instant he took off his hat to step inside, monopolized Ki's attention.

The man was tall, lean, and bowlegged. The hat he doffed had a wide brim, and his pointy boots jangled long-shanked spurs. His red bulb of a nose had been broken and poorly mended, its bridge making a curve under his buckshot eyes, and his nose gave the impression it was smeared across his face. The man was the rider Ki had glimpsed, the killer of Leroy Shaw.

McManus spoke through lips tight and grim. "Word's come that the level of the Vicar's started dropping again"—

he gave a slight, unintentional nod toward the man—"and we all know there's only one cause of that. The Emerald's started construction on their dam again, just like they were ordered not to. It's our move next—"

"What Mr. McManus is saying is," the man interrupted brusquely, "he's decided the Bar M's going to wreck it tonight."

One of the hands muttered, "You can bet Emerald's got that dam guarded night'n day."

"Possibly so," McManus responded, picking up on the comment. "Guards or not, just following the river to their dam, then planting charges and blowing it up will be a dangerous undertaking. But it's a matter of life and death in any case. We must show Emerald we mean business, that they must halt their operations. The Bar M's future, the ranch's very existence, is at stake."

The man grinned toothily. "Now you're talking. Me'n Grosner will be siding you, ready to swap lead. Them jacks can't deny Bar M water rights, and you're only enforcing how the court'll rule."

McManus faced him, scowling. "I'm beginning to suspect, Purdue, the court will uphold Emerald. I'm wondering if I own rights to my land, much less water—if maybe I haven't been somehow bamboozled."

The man named Purdue growled, "Muffle your clapper. Remember you're deep mortgaged, and who to, before you spout accusin'."

The embarrassed punchers stared at their plates. None of them cared to witness dirty laundry being dragged about or to see their boss standing angered and humiliated, acquiescing.

"Anyhow, we have to play the hand we've been dealt," McManus went on after a moment, wiping his fingers together, and then he addressed his foreman, "Sam, check whatever explosives and stuff we've got in stock, and if you figure we'll need more, hie into town this afternoon. Take Fong with you. Claims he's a powderman, and if he's as much a one as he's a fighter, he'll do to have along."

"Not the Chink," Purdue objected, drawn aware of Ki and now glaring suspiciously. "Dunno him, can't place him, but something tells me somewhere once I seen him and didn't like what I seen."

Ki rose to the challenge. "I know my work, and I work for the Bar M," he called in an even, steely tone. "'Less you're an owner, it makes no difference if you love me or not." His voice softened then, becoming more courteous. "Mr. McManus, I drew cards in your game when I signed on, you told me so yourself. I'll blast that dam for you and take my chances on collecting my wages."

"You're elected, Fong," McManus confirmed, lashing a defiant glance at Purdue before surveying the packed cookhouse. "Believe me, I regret it having come to this, locking horns with the Emerald, with a widow woman. Regret her husband passing, too; he wasn't a bad egg for a logger. But I'm left no choice."

He pivoted without another word and stalked outside. Purdue followed, after first giving Ki a parting glower, his brow thunderous.

A gloomy pall descended on the cookhouse. Men toyed with their food, brooding or staring off into space, until Ledbetter stood up and banged a fork on his tin cup for attention.

"I know what you're all thinking," he stated. "I don't like raw feuding, either. But if we're going to hold to our beefs and handle our jobs, we've got to fight for the Bar M."

At the far end of the table, a puncher cleared his throat

and spoke up. "Goes without saying, Sam. We're willing to ride for Mr. McManus. What galls me is bucking lead to defend a ranch that, in truth, belongs to Vince Freis."

"We take our orders from Mac," Ledbetter hedged. "What I'm driving at, is you're all on my list for pickin' to tackle the dam. Any galoot who's concerned with going can draw his time and pack here'n now. I want no one runnin' on me if Emerald gets wind and starts slinging bullets."

The men waited, saying nothing. Their foreman had declared himself in on the raid, and on every face Ki read testimony to the loyalty and regard he commanded. When the long silence had run its course, Ledbetter nodded somberly and sat back down.

The lunch session soon broke up, the hands returning to their tasks. Ki went with Ledbetter to inspect the ranch's blasting supplies, which were kept safely distant in a junky shed.

The inventory turned up a meager store. There were a few caps and coils of double-tape fuse, a rusted fuse cutter and crimper, and the dregs of a keg of No. 3 black powder. Shelved apart were cans of No. 5 powder, along with a shiny metal loading tool and boxes of wads, shot, and similar odds and ends.

What there was told Ki a lot. Someone here had a choke-bore shotgun and liked making shells for it. But the age, neglect, and lack of supplies indicated the Bar M rarely used explosives. So Purdue had scrounged what he could, choosing the can of the No. 5 for convenience or out of ignorance, and he had carried off his takings wrapped in waxed paper, as though concealing a theft.

The implications were clear: McManus and his crew knew nothing as yet about yesterday's attack and Leroy Shaw's death. But the enraged loggers up at the Emerald

106

had pinned Purdue's crime on the Bar M. McManus was ordering a foray tonight that would trespass deep into Emerald territory, straight into the sights of avenging guns. And Ki could not inform him without exposing his cover.

Ledbetter raked his beard. "What'cha think, Fong?"

"Not enough here to blow a good fart," Ki retorted disdainfully. "We'll need more kegs, a cranker, some elec—"

"Whup! Save it for Grenfeld when we get to his hard-ware."

They departed the shed and headed toward the stable, only to be stopped midway by a hand with a problem. Diverted, the foreman said to Ki, "Go have the wagon readied. I'll catch up in a jiffy."

Ki continued to the stable where he had left his roan before lunch and told the hostler what was wanted. Taking advantage of Ledbetter's delay, he borrowed paper and pencil and hastily wrote a brief note to Margot, sketching the situation and asking for restraint. He tucked the note in a vest pocket, having no idea how he could relay it to her, but feeling there was no other possibility open to avoid the imminent bloodbath.

The hostler finished hitching the one-horse wagon, then Ledbetter arrived, and they rode out across the yard. From the porch of the main house, McManus gave a parting wave as he stood talking with Purdue. Ledbetter tugged his hat in a deferential salute, but Ki perceived a hostility in the foreman.

Waiting until they passed the gate and were rolling along at a steady clip, Ki remarked casually, "Who's that fellow, the one who disliked me at lunch? He sure seems to pull drag with Mr. McManus."

Ledbetter shot Ki a glance and made a wry grimace.

"Justin Purdue. He's one of Marshal Freis' toadies."

"Deputies, you mean?"

"You can call them that, but they're still thugs."

"He does have the look of a gunnie, at that. The sort of showoff who notches pistol grips. What's he do at that Bar M?"

"Eat and play solitaire. Purdue's not under my orders and not on the Bar M payroll, far's I know. For some reason, maybe some deal with Freis, Mac keeps him and at times Rube Grosner on the spread, and it plumb ain't for good looks." Ledbetter shrugged his shoulders expressively. "I've not seen Purdue in action, but he may get his chance to show any fancy skills off at the dam tonight."

That was about all Ki could pry out of Ledbetter. The rest of the trip was generally spent in silent contemplations.

Sweetgum seemed to be lazily dozing in the bright haze of afternoon. Ki appeared to be similarily relaxed as they entered the town, but inwardly he was tense, his eyes sweeping the walks and rails along the straggling main street. One of the first items to catch his interest was a big hand-lettered poster tacked to the bulletin board fronting the law office:

REWARD * $100 * REWARD
MISS JESSICA STARBUCK
WANTED FOR MURDER AND FLIGHT
TO AVOID PROSECUTION
CONTACT MARSHAL VINCENT Q. FREIS,
SWEETGUM, OREGON

Ki regarded the sign with contempt. It was a cheap trick. Jessie was worth more than a hundred bucks—but then, the reward was likely coming from Freis, not from the state coffers.

Ledbetter pulled in by a hitchrail near GRENFELD'S HARDWARE & EMPORIUM. As they began walking toward it, Ki noticed the Biggses' covered wagon parked near the land office farther down the street. Wearing a polka dot dress, Rachel sat holding slack reins. Waiting for Duncan, Ki presumed, and just bored enough to gaze about and see him. He kept a watch on her movements as he tried to make himself invisible.

With unerring instinct, Rachel shifted and looked straight at Ki. Beaming, she opened her mouth to call out a greeting.

Snatching Ledbetter by the arm and twisting him around so his back was to Rachel, Ki gestured and yelled, "Don't step there!"

"What?" Ledbetter blundered to and fro. "Where?"

While keeping Ledbetter momentarily distracted, Ki glanced at Rachel, shaking his head with a finger to his lips in a shushing signal. Quizzical and a bit hurt, she nodded and feigned indifference.

Ledbetter turned on Ki with whiskers bristling. "Well?"

"I thought I saw a snake."

"A snake! You're scared hysterical by snakes?"

"No, I trap them for medicine."

"You foreign gents are daft!" Sputtering, Ledbetter led as they continued to the hardware store.

Sitting along the store's platform walkway were three men, timberjacks, whom Ki recognized as belonging to Emerald. They'd been conversing, but ceased on seeing Ki and Ledbetter approach.

"Uh-oh," Ledbetter murmured, "Pay them no heed, Fong."

Ki intended otherwise. Hooking his fingers in his vest

pockets, he passed Ledbetter and strutted pugnaciously to the platform. The jacks obeyed orders and studiously ignored him. Ki was appreciating their obedience when the door opened and Bjorn came out with a package under his arm.

Ki brushed into him, shouldering him and jostling hard. "Hell!" Bjorn barked, startled.

He stumbled with Bjorn, turned, and pressed his palms high against Bjorn's meaty chest and swiped downward, as if initially wanting to shove Bjorn away and thinking better of it. "Watch where you're going!"

"Yeu, I do not know yeu, stranger," Bjorn said politely.

"And don't do it again," Ki snapped, heading through the open door. "If you're blind, get a dog. If you're just lost, maybe you should take along maps—and instructions—in your pocket."

Ledbetter followed, chased by muttered expletives. "We coulda been massa-creed, Fong!" He clawed at his beard. "I ain't riskin' shoppin' with you never no more!"

"You overexcite," Ki said blandly.

A young clerk intervened and promptly was sent to bring Mr. Grenfeld, who proved to be a gregarious chap in a green apron. While Grenfeld and Ki huddled over explosives, the clerk filled Ledbetter's mundane requests for coffee, beans, and other staples, together with quantities of various ammunition. To Ki's disappointment, Grenfeld had everything he needed: four six-pound canisters of No. 1 powder, suitable for blasting very hard rock, ore, and partially built dams; a dynamo blaster box with assorted fuses and spools of leader and connecting wire; rope, crimpers, augers, picks, and anything else that seemed useful.

All four men labored to load the wagon, and Ledbetter

predicted the horse would drop dead trying to pull it. "Least them loggers have long left," he grumbled, mounting the seat, "and can't hoot'n beller."

About to climb aboard, Ki saw Duncan emerge from the land office. Ki ducked and Ledbetter peered querulously at him.

Duncan wore clean duds and his cartridge belt crossing his chest. But he now packed a percussion Starr .44 in a scuffed leather holster slung on his bandolier. It looked cumbersome, but looks could mislead. Ki feared that Duncan would see him.

Duncan, though, was focusing on his niece, smiling broadly as he strode to their wagon. "Got the paper," Ki heard him exclaim, patting his hip pocket. "We're filed, Rachel, we—"

"Hold it right there, Duncan Biggs!"

The strident voice of Marshal Freis speared the air, cutting off Duncan and pinning him next to the front wagon wheel. Predictably, such a lawman's command also drew the interest of passersby, who turned to view the marshal trotting down the street from his office with Deputy Bruno, whose head was adorned with a turban of bandages.

"You're under arrest," Freis declared, bracing Duncan, "on charges of aiding and abetting a prisoner to escape custody."

Rachel let out a low cry of alarm. Freis leveled an accusing finger at her uncle as if it were a gun. From across the street, Ki watched tensely, hands in his vest pockets ready to help Duncan and to hell with Ulysses Fong. But Duncan didn't appear to need help; after the first slight flush of shock, he rallied with mocking eyes and a challenging grin. "Prove it."

Grimacing, Bruno gestured angrily at his bandages.

111

"I'm wearing the proof! That Starbuck gal conked me over the noggin with my own gun, and she got my gun by pulling that hide-out gun you sneaked her. C'mon, let's lock him in the jug."

Duncan, shaking his head, backed a pace to block Freis' hand and elude Bruno's grab for his revolver. "Now, you hold it!" His mocking grin soured into a defiant frown as he objected, "I won't submit to arrest without due process of law. I'm a property owner as of today and won't be harassed as if I were some drifter."

"Yeah, property gained o'er the bones of your poor daddy. It takes a two-faced polecat to want to go off with his killer."

"Vile slander—beneath even you." Duncan swelled with righteous indignation. "Marshal, your deputy dunce is a liar, desperate to cover some fool bungle of his own, like forgetting to lock the cell. If you believe his scurrilous lie, if you think you can prove Miss Starbuck needed me to escape this cretin, swear out a warrant and serve me legally. Otherwise, leave me in peace."

Freis hesitated, eyeing Duncan and gauging his resistance, then glancing around as if counting witnesses. After blistering Bruno with an oath, he growled at Duncan, "All right, Biggs—for now. Mark me, if I do get the goods on you, you'll be due processed so fast, it'll make your head swim." Freis pivoted and stalked off up the street to disappear inside his office with a hard slam of his door.

Bruno gazed after Freis, then cursing savagely, jerked off his tin star and flung it aside. "You and me got a score to settle, Biggs!" he snarled. "You got a gun. Let's see you use it."

Duncan paused in the act of climbing into the wagon. There was no fear on his face as he saw Bruno go into a gunslinger's crouch, his fingers hovering inches from his Colt. "I want no trouble with you," he said calmly and turned his back on Bruno, starting to climb the hub of the front wheel.

Rachel's terrified scream warned Duncan, brought him whirling around in time to glimpse Bruno draw his revolver, aiming for a pointblank shot at Duncan's back. With a swiftness from naturally quick reflexes and intense practice, Duncan drew with the back of his hand against his body, corkscrewing his .44 out in an arc up and across his chest.

His shot blended with Bruno's, but the deputy's bullet smashed into the hickory wheel inches from Duncan's midriff. Bruno tried to re-aim, to fire again, but the heavy Colt slipped from his lax fingers as he swayed on his feet. He clutched at his chest, where a scarlet blossom stained his shirt. Then, with a gagging exhalation, Bruno buckled at the knees and pitched sideward to the dirt, his boots kicking up the dust.

The gunfray had begun and ended so fast that Ki found himself with a dagger in hand and no Bruno to throw it at. Sliding it back into his vest, he glanced at Ledbetter to see if the foreman had detected his movements, but Ledbetter was staring at Biggs' wagon, as were the other spectators. More people were converging, draining from stores and saloons to encircle the dead deputy. And Ki likewise saw the law office door bat open as Marshal Freis burst outside, lifting a Winchester .44-40 saddle carbine to his cheek, aiming carefully.

The smoke produced by Duncan's percussion revolver was still fogging the air. Duncan squinted through the haze and, perceiving the marshal had the drop on him, lowered his weapon.

A townsman hastily shouted out, "Twenty witnesses,

113

Marshal, twenty of us saw your deputy try to drill that feller in the back."

"Bruno was backshootin'," another yelled.

"I'll testify to it," a third cried. "Think about it."

Freis paused, thinking about it, and relaxed his stance.

"Be happy to stand trial, Marshal," Duncan then called, holstering his revolver. "In a regular courtroom, not a kangaroo deal. Well, time's wastin'. You'll make sure this carrion gets due burial, won't you?"

Before Freis could frame a reply, Duncan climbed into the wagon and took the reins from his niece. He swung his team about, the wagon describing a tight loop around the corpse sprawled on the dusty street and then straightening to trundle up the street. Freis, swearing, pouched his carbine again and followed Duncan with the sight, holding his desire to trigger in check with a visible effort. Duncan gave no indication he knew or cared about the threat, except, perhaps, a sardonic chuckle as he drove past Freis, churning on out of town and vanishing in a wake of dust.

Smiling wryly, Ki got into the Bar M wagon.

"Flabbergasting," Ledbetter said. "Can you believe? Freis, tied and shorn. One of his mad dogs downed while frothing. By a hayseed, to boot."

Ledbetter rambled on. Ki heard but didn't listen, his attention shifting from what had happened to what would.

And Ki worried. He worried Bjorn would ignore his hint and overlook the instructions palmed on him. Or Bjorn would fail to poke in his pockets for something else and miss chancing on the note in time. Or if the message got to Margot, she'd reject his pleas. Or when she shared his information with her jacks, they'd gather on their own at the dam and turn it into a slaughter.

The future of this night looked stacked, rigged against

fragile hope. One way or another, what would happen was bound to be bloody: wounds to treat, graves to dig, and calls for continued fighting. Events had progressed too far for him, or Jessie, or anybody to stop the clock of destiny.

And that's what really worried Ki.

Chapter 11

The previous night, while Ki had stayed on Margot's soft sofa, Jessie had camped out on the Biggses' hard ground.

She had declined their offer to share Zack's cabin, it being only one room. Moreover, it seemed to her that Duncan was becoming increasingly aware of her as a woman, although outwardly he continued acting the courteous, proper gentleman. And in turn, she sensed her awareness of his masculinity. For all their polite behavior, an undercurrent of attraction was budding between them, so Jessie refused to sleep that close to Duncan, fearing they already had enough problems.

She spread her bedroll a short distance away in a boulder-ringed grassy clearing fed by a brook. There, too, the wagon had been parked and the horses staked out—though they were way across from Jessie—by a pond formed by the brook before exiting through the far side's rocks.

Awake at dawn, Jessie saddled her borrowed mare, strapped on the bags, and left without telling Duncan or Rachel. She'd warned them she'd likely be gone and not to expect her back till evening, perhaps after their trip to Sweetgum.

She headed for Grants Pass, riding at a sustained lope that covered the miles without overtaxing her horse. Arriving in late morning, she spent until early afternoon in a flurry of activity. Most of the money she deposited in the Grants Pass Bank & Trust, which was sufficiently large to know the Starbuck name. She avoided the local law, concerned about possible ties to Marshal Freis, telegraphing instead a coded report to her company lawyers at Salem, the capital, requesting assistance and the state's intercession. Next, she met with the area superintendent of the Oregon & California Railroad, which owned the land that Emerald had leased. Finally she reloaded the saddlebags with supplies, added to her saddle a new scabbard and Winchester carbine, and then departed Grants Pass at a road-eating, steady gait.

Upon reaching the cabin quite late in the afternoon, Jessie found that Duncan and Rachel had not yet returned from Sweetgum. That was dandy by her, she thought, as she went to the clearing; she was sun-broiled and dust-caked and needed a little time to clean up. First, though, she had to care for her horse, which was lathered as if by shaving soap. Afterward she stripped naked and waded into the pond, alert for anyone's approach, her revolver handy atop her clothes on the bank.

The shock of cold mountain water momentarily robbed Jessie of breath, but brought blood pulsing back into her wearily aching body. She washed with a cake of glycerin soap she'd bought in Grants Pass, and after scrubbing herself from neck on down, she sat low to cleanse her face and shampoo her hair. She was just swinging up from having ducked under to rinse off when she thought she heard horses and a wagon down by the cabin.

Not waiting to confirm the noises, Jessie sprang from the water. If she were imagining things, she could always get back in; if it were the Biggses, as she suspected, she had no intention of being caught immodestly squatting in a pool; and if it were somebody else, she had no intention of being caught defenseless as well as nude. Hastily snatching her revolver and clothes, she sprinted for the rocks, breasts swaying. She pranced with spritely grace to avoid stepping on occasional nettles.

The sounds grew louder as Jessie scrambled through a crevice and dipped behind the boulders. She had managed to leave her boots behind, but as it was, she scarcely had time to thrust on her pants and blouse before somebody entered the clearing and reined in.

"Hello, what's this?" she heard, recognizing the voice an instant before she peered around the edge of the crevice. She saw Duncan on his wagon, staring down at her boots and then gazing about. "Jessie? Hey, Jessie, it's only us; we're back."

"Be right there, Duncan," she called. Swiftly she wadded her lacy unmentionables in her back pockets, stuck her revolver in her belt, and eased from the crevice looking as composed as possible, combing her fingers through her wet hair and tucking in her blouse.

He regarded her padding barefoot toward him, and the fattest damn grin Jessie could remember receiving lit up his face. "Well, now," he drawled, and she knew he had reconstructed exactly what had happened. "Came to unhitch, is all, and tell you Rachel will have supper ready in about an hour. Ah, you want a towel? There're some in a trunk in back. C'mon up and dry off back there."

"Might as well." She placed a foot on the front wheel hub to hoist herself up, Duncan taking her outstretched hand to help. Her toes slipped; she lurched, but Duncan's grip held and he boosted her somewhat ungainly into the wagon with him. Unbalanced, Jessie fell against his chest, wincing as she struck the hard iron of his bandolier-slung holstered revolver. She felt his strong hands on her sides while he tried to support her—then, as their faces brushed together, the moist pressure of his lips when he kissed her.

She gasped, "Duncan!"

"I've wanted to do that," he said. "I didn't know it until now, but that's why I'm here, Jessie, because I wanted to kiss you."

Even as he spoke, Jessie realized he was admitting his inner truth. Worse, it was triggering a response within her, an intriguing tingle worming up through her flesh, and she tried to resist, to wriggle from his arms. But somehow she only drew closer, her damp breasts pressing against his broad chest.

"No," she whispered and she jerked her head aside when his mouth touched hers again. "T–tell me about what happened today."

Duncan chuckled. "Well, for one, you're now officially a fugitive from *in*justice with your own wanted poster and reward."

"Don't joke," she said with a shiver. "Did you see Ki?"

"Rachel did. Told me he was with some cowboy and he signaled her not to show she knew him. Some timberjacks out front of a store acted likewise, she said, so we kinda figure Ki's pulling a fast one with Emerald's complicity. Me, I was up to my ars—er, armpits filing probates and property documents, and—oh, yeah, Bruno backshot at me and I killed him."

"Bruno and you did *what?*" Jessie gaped astounded, so Duncan repeated his remark and filled in the details. When he was done, Jessie heaved a sigh. "Freis daren't let you get away with it if he hopes to keep others cowed.

He must hit back soon, maybe by ambushing, but more likely in a way to make an example of you. Duncan, don't waste any time worrying about my side of this. If Freis comes here, it'll be with the idea of wiping you and Rachel off the face of the earth."

"Hell, it's worth the risk just to hear you worrying about me," he replied, putting his fingers on her cheek and gently, firmly, turning her face to kiss her.

Jessie leaned against him and accepted the kiss without really returning it, merely allowing it, feeling his embrace around her, feeling his hands tenderly press and caress. His was a touch of respect, of affection, of questioning exploration, and she could feel his heart. It pounded against her breast, and she could feel its beat matching the pulse of her own quickening heart.

"Don't," she whispered, making that required attempt to stop it—for his sake, for her sake. The complications. "Don't start."

"I'll not start anything I can't finish." And, with an insistence that implied he knew enough about women to know when *no* meant *yes* he quieted her with his eager lips.

Jessie lost herself in his kiss, her resistance weakening. The tip of his tongue flickered to touch hers, and she felt a convulsive shudder pass through him, and it melted her. Her arms, having a will of their own, went around him and hugged the muscles tensing in his back— his masculine torso tightening in a quick, reflexive movement. The glow of desire was strong in her.

Sensing the last of her reserve fade away, Jessie surrendered to him in that moment. Her body was alive in the tight bands of his arms as slowly, gently, Duncan shifted them backward off the wagon seat, through the canvas flap, and to the bed of the wagon. There was more room here, enough cargo having been taken into the cabin last night to leave a narrow space along the floorboards. There, for a long moment, they pressed torso to torso. Then Duncan disengaged slightly, just sufficiently to remove his bandolier and Jessie's pistol, tossing them aside as they both moved to come closer, more intimate in their renewed embrace.

He eased her down and put her back on the bare, rough wood of the wagon bed. Jessie cocked one knee up. Duncan lay on his stomach beside her, his tongue a lance of fire in her mouth, his hand moving to enclose one taut, unbound breast. His kneading fingers felt so natural, so good to Jessie that she let the erotic thrill sweep through her without questioning. It was equally natural that she yearned to feel his body, seeking that culminating position as she tugged his shirt and pants and opened her legs to him. He was firm and hard and trim and fitted nicely between her hips as she centered him in the cradle of her pelvic mound.

Weak moaning sounds arose in her throat when, after a short interval, he shifted to one side and stroked his fingers down from her breasts to rub teasingly her sensitive delta. Her hand found his bulge, closed, felt him large, hard, ready. He quivered in pleasure at her touch. Finally he crouched to undress.

She eyed him apprehensively. "Somebody might come."

"That, Jessie, is the whole idea."

"You know what I mean."

"I don't care, do you?"

She didn't answer at once, absorbed by how his big hands were being careful as they fumbled with her clothing. She felt cooling evening air on her midriff as her blouse was bunched up above her breasts. Not helping him any, she let him lift her to slip the blouse over her head. When he opened the fly of her jeans, she murmured, "No, I imagine I don't," and she raised her buttocks to let him skin her pants down slowly, exposing the plane of her lower abdomen, then her golden-red curls.

"I've wanted you since we met, Jessie."

"I know, Duncan."

Lying naked, she watched avidly as he stripped and returned to her. She felt her legs open with a touch of his hands, wanting it now, unashamed, her blood singing.

Duncan's fingers explored her tenderly, massaged her, then quested lower and inside while he hunkered with his face between her splayed creamy thighs. He kissed deep between her fleshy lips, replacing his finger with his laving tongue. She felt him thirsting to take her, hungry to possess her. Jessie let her body accept his lust with a fresh feeling of abandon, a frenzy of motion. She spread her legs wider and undulated her buttocks up against his greedy ministrations.

She climaxed swiftly, feeling the clenching fist deep up inside her belly, although it was over in brief moments of moaning and fevered bliss. Yet even as her senses were concentrating in chronic spasm, she felt Duncan rising, looming over her full length. Her trembling thighs arched to meet his thrusting hips. She took his erection in hand, sighed with anticipation, poised her buttocks, and inserted him, feeling herself part smoothly as he eased his weight down on her, penetrating her and surging deep into her, body and soul.

Jessie panted for him. She helped, hoisting her bottom up and pressing against him until he was inside as far as he could go. And seething with the fill of him, feeling engorged, she wished to keep him there as a part of her.

She bowed upward under him and dug her heels in.

He began pumping and she gasped aloud, her breath spewing harshly. All of her nerves seemed to be wrapped around his hammering probe. He cupped her rump, pressing her buttocks as she bucked lovingly against his strokes. She swallowed him deeper as she raised both legs, cocking them up, and her heels pushed against the wagon floor. She felt herself spiraling toward a second orgasm.

When she peaked with moans and sucking kisses, and her insides convulsed tightly around his pistoning shaft, she felt him lunging deep, shoving hard, stiffening. He cried out, releasing a thundering burst within her, flooding her.

Limply they lay together. His mouth was sweet, no longer demanding. He remained in her, relaxing atop her, partially supported on one elbow. He said, "P'raps we should go. Rachel, y'know. And I'm hungry."

She squirmed a little under him. "Strange, I'm full."

"Seconds?"

"Thank you, I've already had them."

"Let me know if you want a snack later."

Soon, all too soon, they reluctantly slipped from their bond and dressed. Jessie helped Duncan unhitch and care for the wagon horses, then walked with him to the cabin for dinner.

The fare was simple, mainly bread and a stew with a little of everything in it, but a lot of it. Conversation centered on the day's activities, Rachel chattily embellishing their adventures in Sweetgum, while Jessie laconically edited her experiences in Grants Pass. By the end of the meal, Jessie felt the reward poster was more of an irritating hazard than an impending danger; agreed that Ki was up to some flimflam, with the Bar M as his probable dupe; and was convinced that Marshal Freis posed the gravest, most immediate threat, quite likely at the head of some thugs.

"The chips are down," she stated flatly, wanting to emphasize the serious peril the Biggses faced. "Freis could send a gang raiding any night, including tonight. You haven't planted crops or built homes yet, but his objective still would be to destroy what you do have— Zack's cabin, the wagon and team, and your lives with them."

Duncan patted his revolver. "We'll be prepared."

"Trapped is a better word." She glanced around at the walls. "This place would burn. A stock of water should be laid in."

Jessie's suggestion was so sensible that when they took their plates and cooking utensils to the pond for washing they brought along extra pots and jugs to fill with water. A few more treks were made, one with the empty stew cauldron, to secure a good supply in case any attackers tried to torch them out. They left the horses and wagon there, not knowing a more protective spot in the gulch, and on the last trip, Jessie got her new carbine and the additional rounds of ammunition she'd brought back from Grants Pass.

Night had fallen by now, which made her all the more uneasy. She listened at the door and watched the stars glitter in the canopy of surrounding trees, and after satisfying herself she didn't hear or see anything untoward, she closed the door. "I'd feel a lot easier, Rachel, if you and your uncle would go stay in Grants Pass till the worst of it blows over."

"We don't figure to start new lives here without having to fight for them," Rachel declared stoutly. "I don't doubt some blood may be shed, but we're sticking pat." She yanked a towel out of a box beneath one of the bunks,

125

grabbed a Model '67 Winchester, and went to the door. "I am going for a dip," she announced and ducked outside, closing the door firmly behind her.

Duncan chuckled. "Biggs women stand by their kinfolk to the last shot, Jessie. With her kind of spunk, we can't lose."

"I fear the odds don't make courage a sure bet."

"Often bucking long is the only way to win."

For a long while Jessie said nothing. Neither did Duncan, who sat patiently cleaning the dead ferryman's rifle with a ramrod and cloth. At last he raised the rifle to the light, and while sighting through its bore, he remarked, "Has to do with percentages of risk to reward. Well, hell, I'm a gambler."

"A reformed one, according to Rachel. But after your jailhouse performance last night, I'd have sworn you were a gospel minister."

"Minister's son. Paw was once a travelin' preacher, Bible in one hand, pistol in the other. Despite the upbringin', or maybe account of it, me'n Thurlow grew into hellacious black sheep, the scourge of any parents. Us, I guess, and Paw's roamings are what drove Maw to run off with a salesman. Course, she weren't no true Biggs. Still, it nie busted Paw, heart and soul."

"That's when he gave up preaching, was it?"

"When the Lord speaks, you do His bidding. When it seems He's lost His voice, you still keep your ears peeled, but turn your body to workin' busy at what you must. Paw, now, he reckoned a change—"

"Shh!" Jessie, intentionally stationed by the open window, concentrated. Sure enough, she heard the muffled drum of hoofbeats from somewhere up the gulch, toward the wagon road. The pale moonlight failed to penetrate the gloom underneath the treees, yet even if she couldn't identify the riders by sight, Jessie had no doubts they were none other than Marshal Freis' gunmen.

"Trouble's coming," she said. "Douse the lamps quick!"

Duncan leaped to a table lamp, then a bracket lamp, blowing down their chimneys. Then he crossed to Jessica to peer out, his eyes following the line of her pointing arm. The riders remained totally invisible until they reached the outskirts of the cabin clearing, and then they were merely blobs of hard black against the slightly softer black of the background. The riders halted and snatches of low-voiced conversation filtered to the window. In a moment or so the pack separated, drifting at a slow gait to avoid making much noise as they circled the clearing to surround the cabin.

"There's a chunky outline over to the left that reminds me plenty of Freis," Duncan said. He dived across the room, snatching up the rifle and drawing his revolver on the way to the door. "I can't say for sure, but I do know of one who's definitely out there."

"Stay in here," Jessie snapped. "You don't know where Rachel is outside. Your niece will be safe enough if she keeps hidden, which she will."

Sighing, Duncan nodded and rammed the rifle barrel through the slender gunport cut in the door. Jessie turned her attention to the riders, carefully sighted her carbine on a hulking dark shape, and squeezed the trigger. The carbine's report almost drowned out the scream from her target, the shape tumbling to earth.

For a moment, the tableau froze, discovery of their sneaky approach having caught them by surprise. Then Duncan fired through the port, and the riders broke in a concerted rush toward the cabin. An oil-soaked torch blossomed in the night as one of them, leaving his horse, raced on foot and hurled the firebrand to the roof.

Instantly a shot rang out as Duncan, shifting locations, fired his Starr .44 through a chink in the log wall. The torch-wielding gunman, running back to his horse, dropped in his tracks. A sharp salvo of gunfire now burst in the night as the raiders opened fire to avenge the death of one of their number. Their bullets thudded against the roof and walls of the cabin. By the glare of the blazing torch that was igniting the roof, Duncan and Jessie aimed returning blasts at silhouetted riders.

Another gunman spun and fell. Jessie couldn't figure how he'd been hit. Discerning details was very difficult in the morass of swirling shadow and flickering light outside, and vision was worsening as choking, eye-stinging smoke began curling down inside from the smoldering roof shingles. But Jessie knew she hadn't shot, and unless Duncan's old rifle could angle lead around corners, she knew from his position opposite here that he couldn't have shot.

It was also near impossible to detect specific sounds among the chaotic uproar of shouts and gunfire. But it seemed to Jessie that in rapid succession came two deeper reports from some heavier weapon than the raiders were using. The throatier cracks coincided with two more gunmen crumpling violently, blood spluttering from their mortal wounds. Startled curses rippled along the ragged line of raiders. But now, inside the cabin, Jessie realized what must be happening. Rachel, summoned by the ruckus, was darting about with her Winchester '67, boldly sniping at close range, trusting that the confused bedlam of conflict would protect her from discovery.

"Hot damn!" Duncan bolted out the door.

Jessie, standing at the window, judged that Duncan had also surmised the situation, and she first feared he

128

had rushed out in an insane attempt to find his niece. Then Jessie saw what he was up to. She was alarmed as she glimpsed him hurl a ladder against the eaves and scurry up with a cauldron of water.

She yelled a warning, spotted a wedge of riders spearing in to riddle Duncan while he stood up there, an open target at easy range. Levering and firing as fast as she could, she heard the harsh snap of his percussion pistol from above her. And from out of nowhere stabbed the blasts of Rachel's Winchester. The combined defense routed the chargers, smashing one from his saddle and wounding two others before the raiders could retreat to the concealing fringe of the clearing. As they tried to reorganize for a second attack, Duncan doused the blaze, scrambled down the ladder, and sprinted safely back inside.

"Helluva risk, but it was either show myself or have the cabin roast round our heads," he panted, barricading the door. He took a moment to rearm his revolver. Then he joined Jessie in renewing gunfire.

Outside, the gunmen were increasingly faltering in disarray. They had not expected such fierce resistance. Nor had they expected to be caught in a crossfire, snagged between the cabin and someone stalking behind them and picking them off with unerring lead.

That Winchester materialized again with a fiery discharge, only to vanish phantomlike as another raider keeled earthward. Inside the cabin, Jessie and Duncan let loose a barrage whenever they saw the fleeting shadow of a rider among the dark trees around the clearing. The once-smug gang fought stubbornly, then desperately, finally crumbling into pandemonium, until Jessie heard the voice of one gunnie shout loudly, "Pull out! We're losing too many!"

The raiders broke away and began galloping pell-mell for the path that led to the wagon road, their flanks harried by raking shots until they were out of gun range.

As the receding hoofbeats faded away, a strange hush descended around the clearing, broken only by the erratic neighing of horses. In a few minutes the door hinges squeaked, and Duncan edged out to the porch, crouching with revolver in hand.

Nothing disturbed the quiet.

"They're gone, Jessie. It may be a trick."

Jessie stepped to the corner and was warily eyeing along the side of the cabin when they heard a rustling of undergrowth a little beyond the clearing. They couldn't tell if it was from a raider sneaking on foot, or one of the milling horses, or what, until Rachel's voice snapped, "Oh, those dirty brutes!"

"Get back there, gal!" Duncan called. "We can't be sure they didn't leave men behind to trap us!"

"All right, Uncle Dunc, I—ugh!" There was some soft thrashing of brush, but then that died away and all was peaceful again.

Duncan craned forward, puzzled. "Rachel?"

A long pause.

Duncan stood, perplexity becoming anxiety. "Rachel!"

Another wait.

Duncan glanced at Jessie, and they both broke into a mad dash toward the area from which they'd last heard her. Under the murky curtain of trees they plunged—swatting a horse aside, thrusting on through thick foliage, Duncan frantically yelling Rachel's name.

"Here," Jessie said, coming upon a tamped pocket in some bushes. "She must've been hiding here when she was answering you."

"Then what became of her?" he demanded querulously.

As if on cue, a man's voice shouted from somewhere further on, deeper in the gulch. His voice was a callous baritone, but Jessie couldn't identify it as that of anyone in particular, distance and forest blurring it. His words, though, were clear. "I got the sweetie, you hear me?"

"You shitty bastard! Hurt one hair on her—!"

"Good, you hear me. I'll trade your live niece for them dead beaver pelts. You got till sundown tomorrow to bring 'em or directions to 'em to the ol' prospector's shanty on Wapato Gorge."

"I dunno where they're hid!" Duncan roared.

"Bullcrap. One day—or Thurlow's brat ends like him."

"How do I know she's okay? Let her talk!"

"Afraid she's havin' a forced siesta right now." Raucously laughing, the man could be heard running away. Then came the faint whicker of a horse, followed by hoofbeats crashing off into the woods.

An expression of loathing and fury gnarled Duncan's face. "Didn't recognize the bastard's voice, but five spots you fifty he was Freis," he snarled. "C'mon, hurry, we've got to stop him!"

Heartsick as she felt over the cruel kidnapping, Jessie restrained Duncan. "Don't even try," she pleaded. "Freis, or whoever, will know where he's taking Rachel. We don't. We'll waste the night tracking and never catch up, and we don't have time to spare."

"Spare for what? Goin' to the law? That'd be a waste," he retorted cynically. "Rootin' up the furs? That'd take a miracle."

Jessica thought. "Duncan, do you have a map of the area?"

131

"Yeah, a poor one I bought in town today."

"Hopefully it'll show Wapato Gorge. The kidnapper will go there tomorrow for his ransom, so where better to wait and nab him?"

"That could be anywhere."

"By the way he said it, *the* shanty *on* Wapato Gorge, I suspect it must be fairly unique and stands above the gorge, not down in it. And do you recall, Duncan, what I told you Zack had been raving?"

Duncan reflected, then snapped his fingers. "Wapato Gorge! Somehow, for some reason, Paw'd connected it with Thurlow and the pelts. But then why hadn't he just gone there months earlier?"

"Maybe he had. He obviously knew the location of their cache. Or maybe he couldn't, the gorge being too rough for a man of his age to've managed, so he'd stayed behind while Thurlow trapped there. Maybe he was only dreaming about your brother, when he'd hunted there last, say, or where your father suspected Thurlow'd been waylaid. No, the only thing we can be pretty sure of is that the kidnapper will go there."

"Well, Jessie, so will we. Tonight."

Jessie started to add something, then paused, glimpsing the metal barrel of Rachel's discarded rifle. She went and retrieved it, then gazed high above the growth of trees hemming them in. The moon was like the eye of a corpse floating in the inky blackness of the Oregon sky. She then said, "I've got an odd hunch that we might just find something of interest in Wapato Gorge—after we make sure Rachel is safe."

Chapter 12

Hours later, a midnight moon shed its ethereal light over nine riders en route — with explosives — to Emerald's unfinished dam.

Leery of moonglow that could give them away, McManus kept his squad to the concealing groves and boulders that flanked the Vicar. They advanced upriver slowly and cautiously to avoid alerting any roving nighthawks, yet they numbered enough to overpower the anticipated few dam guards and to buck attacks by some unexpected force. Or so everybody assured one another.

Ki sensed a brooding disquiet in the crewmen. Each face, including Ledbetter's, registered the stubborn fatalism of men who feared they were riding to die — and for a cause that did not have their complete approval. Yet ride they would, although only their cowboy vanity and fidelity to their ranch, Ki suspected, prevented them from calling for their time and quitting the Bar M en masse.

Their boss, of course, was stuffed with bravado. Convinced his survival was in jeopardy and egged on by Freis, McManus couldn't be blamed entirely for striking before being stricken. Unaware Emerald had been struck and the jacks enraged—as none there knew better than Ki—McManus had no idea this try at sabotage could result in a massacre. Yet Ki, while hoping wildly it still might be possible to prevent bloodshed, held his tongue, sure he wouldn't be believed and unsure how firm a grip Freis had on McManus.

And naturally Freis had a henchman along. Not Justin Purdue, who for some reason had missed the ride. It was his other lackey, Rube Grosner, a heavy man who liked hitching at his sagging shell belts, as if to draw attention to his twin pistols. A guy couldn't be around Grosner for five minutes without knowing he relied on those weapons as well as his hulking strength. Like Purdue, it was obvious Grosner was an outcast, a pariah to the Bar M crew.

Almost two more hours of riding in silence brought them to the edge of the heavy timber where Emerald's jacks had logged off vast tracts of land. But they saw no sign of jacks themselves. Indeed, they had penetrated into the heart of the Emerald domain without glimpsing a single guard on patrol when, emerging from the forest, they rode out where the moonlight turned the surrounding terrain into a spectral sculpture of shadow and silver.

Ahead and a tad below their vista, they beheld a lake—or rather, the promise of a lake. It was cupped in a crescent of bare, towering ridges, their slopes spilling steeply, tightly, funneling to form a deep ravine, whose base had once served as a river bed. The Vicar continued flushing thunderously, but now its egress was partially blocked, so it unsuccessfully kept trying to flood the ravine.

"Well, there's the dam," McManus commented, reining in. "I can see now that if ever Emerald got it completed, it'd take triple the charges we brought with us and then some."

He about summed it up, Ki thought. What was built of the dam was akin to some monstrous pier jutting out from the ravine's bank and disrupting the already turbulent flow of water. Looking crude and temporary, it was exceedingly solid, constructed as it was of massive firs felled across the narrowest point along the ravine, where the river dropped over a ledge. Earthen banks had been caved in behind the logs, and huge boulders had been sunk until they piled up like a jetty, buttressing the foundation.

And this was one instance where too much was scarcely enough. The dam was constantly being assailed—pressured by a savage backwash swelling high and buffeting under; scoured by a treacherous riptide raking sidelong and hurtling around the unfinished end, where it pooled in with undammed currents and arced plunging from the ledge just beyond. Ki could see clouds of mist rising from the ravine beneath the waterfall, hear the ominous sound of a torrential downpour.

That sound never would be totally stifled, Ki knew, for the completed dam would need spillways along its rim for the inevitable overflow. The lake filling up behind it would be sizable and certainly provide sufficient water and force to sluice logs down to the Rogue—if not sling 'em to California. Blasting the dam after it was done would be a disaster; blasting it now would seriously cripple any logging operations for the rest of the summer.

Ki turned from contemplating the dam. McManus was telling the others, "Don't see any guards; don't hear any, either. Be best to play it safe, though, so spread out and snoop around some."

Leaving their horses back in the trees, the crew scattered in search, while McManus directed, Grosner picked teeth, and Ki began unloading the explosives. The crew reassembled quickly, not having found any Emerald men lurking about in the vicinity and looking relieved that there wasn't going to be any fighting.

Ki did not feel as sanguine as they. The lack of any guards or patrols probably meant one of two things: Either Margot hadn't received his note and had logically concluded that a few jacks on night duty couldn't provide enough security to justify their lost workdays; or else the jacks, with or without her, had engineered some sneaky and merciless plan. Ki took another long survey of the whole scene, sensing it was almost too easy, yet deciding if it were a trap, it had better be sprung right quick— because for now he found himself committed to Liam McManus' side and gearing up to attack one of Jessie Starbuck's own companies with a big bang.

McManus approached, smiling. "About ready, Fong?"

Ki nodded. "Three cans should do. Sam, let's go."

Other crewmen volunteered, but Ki declined their offers, the last thing he needed being a traffic jam on the dam. And though there was a passable trail to it, moving explosives down and out there would be a ticklish job. Ledbetter, for all his years, had impressed Ki over this day as having an agility probably derived from long experience as an all-round working foreman.

Rope slings had been fashioned for holding the supplies, and after Ledbetter started for the ravine packing two of the canisters, Ki hefted the third one and the awkward spools of connecting and leading wires. He carefully played out a line of leading wire as he navigated the trail, aware it would've been easier to do this on his return, but wanting the chance to check the lay of the

136

line. Shortly they came to an area that took them to the top of the dam. Now the going was even more difficult, logs lying at every conceivable angle, bark-shorn and water-spray slick.

After some while, Ledbetter advised, "We're near the end, Fong. You'd better make up your mind where— Gawd, whazzat?" Startled, he dislodged a stone that tumbled crashing into the river.

"Easy! No pulling a man out if he falls off," Ki cautioned, glancing down the wall of the slippery bulwark. "What's what?"

"That, over there." Ledbetter pointed toward the thrusting end of a trunk, which was one chunky piece of a haphazard jumble of timbers. Draping in a soft coil across the butt was a length of braided rope, one end craftily tied into a hangman's knot and open noose. "What's it doin' here?"

"A rope? You're scared hysterical of ropes?"

"A noose ain't no snake, you . . . Heh, guess I did spook a mite fast," he admitted sheepishly. "Been pondering alla way to the dam how a timberninny could shoot and blow me to smithereens. P'raps I need a snort, Fong."

Ki grinned impishly as he regarded the rope and then Ledbetter again. "A better cure, Sam, is to blow up the rope. See below it, those niches? Make fine holes for placing our charges."

Ki gently climbed down to the niches, testing each step for footing. When Ki was set, Ledbetter lowered the canisters of powder, which Ki shoved deep. Fuses were next, electric detonation not requiring blasting caps. Ki had to make sure each fuse was two feet longer in length than the hole as he inserted them into the now open canisters.

He attached the fuses on one circuit with connecting wire, then joined up with Ledbetter, where he spliced the twin leads of the connecting wire to the leading wire. He winced inwardly as he joined them. He didn't believe McManus or his crew would be so dumb as to fool with the wire and blaster box up there, and Grosner had shown no enmity toward him; but if Purdue had ridden along, Ki would have never risked stringing the wire first, suspecting Purdue might just create an accident and catch Ki in a blast.

On the way back to the others, Ki inspected the leading wire for tight splices and any kinks. Reaching them, Ledbetter a panting step behind, he took the blaster box to where he'd wrapped the wire around a tree trunk. "Get your horses back here, out of range of flying debris," he said, tightening each wire to a post. "Don't mount them; hold them. We'll be long gone before anyone can get here." He pulled the handle up. "Ready?" Everybody was, so he shoved down.

The three canisters detonated simultaneously.

The explosion hit with thunder and lightning, with a violence that seemed to split the ravine to its core and jolt the earth beneath the nine men. A great, gray mushroom of smoke geysered toward the stars, and a fury of wind bent trees and sang through branches. A rock large as an anvil flew high and descended with a crash into timber. Then there was a long, diminishing rumble as Ki heard the dam crumple and spill itself down across the ravine. It reminded him of the blast that had cost Leroy Shaw his life. He had not anticipated it would be so volcanic.

The men were shouting, rushing to see what had occurred and grinning and laughing with satisfaction at the damage. But that's because they don't know any better,

Ki thought as he peered into the smoke-fluming ravine. The dam appeared worse than it actually was structurally, the bulk of it remaining intact. Only a section at the far end collapsed.

And if he were smart, he'd make sure the men didn't grow wise too soon. "C'mon! We wait, we'll chance being spotted!"

Taking Ki's heed the men headed back to their horses. They were chortling about the dam, and some were on the verge of putting boot to stirrup when the underbrush sprouted rifle muzzles aiming straight at them.

A steely voice called, "Stand pat, cowbirds."

Ki stood along with the rest, recognizing the voice as that of Hans Aubrecht. He heard McManus's sharp intake of breath, saw Ledbetter and three punchers lift arms high, saw one fool panic and claw for his pistol—then heard him squawl in pain as he abruptly clasped his red-smeared hand.

"Idiot," the voice said. "Okay, now unbuckle and shuck."

"Go ahead," McManus ordered. "They've got us." He loosened his shell belt and tossed it in front of him, his men hurrying to copy him. Only when everyone had complied did the wooded foliage start to thrash. Emerald jacks shoved aside their camouflage and emerged. Aubrecht, Gerry Shaw, Bjorn, Maxwell—all eighteen jacks approached, smiling with wolfish pleasure.

Last to appear was Margot Gideon, who strolled toward McManus. "Welcome to the Emerald. To what do we owe the pleasure of your visit?" she purred sarcastically, her carbine glinting in the moonlight.

McManus's face was as bleak as the moonlight, but he came out swinging. "Self-defense, Mrs. Gideon! The court's ordered you to cease and desist operations till our case is settled. Surely that allows me a right to see if you're complying."

"Destroying my dam is self-defense?"

"Yes, a desperate measure. Forced on me by your unremitting threat, your brazen continuation of illegal operations."

Listening to this exchange, Ki now fully understood Margot's opinion of McManus. He had a rich voice that'd be the envy of any orator, and when he was wound up like now, he knew how to command his timbre and big words to influence, if not intimidate. McManus was, in essence, a gasbag.

And Margot was too savvy to be impressed or brow-beaten. She shook her head, pointing her carbine at two firs on each side of the ravine. "See there? It's plain we're fitting guy cables and high leads. But you'd have seen nothing freshly done on the dam, if you'd bothered to look first. Ask my jacks. Since the injunction, we've stuck to culling, thinning, rigging for future operations, no felling timber or bucking logs or building dams."

"You hold the cards, Mrs. Gideon, so what you say is so. But I'm not a fool. I know, for example, the water level of the Vicar River's been dropping, no doubt due to more work on your dam."

"Oh, and how do you know? You've measured it?"

"Eh, not precisely. I have it on authority—"

"Whose authority, Mr. McManus?"

"Justin Purdue's."

"Purdue." Her lip curled. "All right, take this on authority. Yesterday one of my riggers—brother of that man, there—died when Purdue blasted down his spar tree. An eyewitness saw Purdue do it and ride off on a Bar M mount. And Purdue almost works for you, doesn't he?"

Shocked speechless, McManus grew ashen.

Grosner broke the hush with a sneery laugh. "Ma'am, you don't expect Mr. McManus to believe that crap, do you?"

"Why not? Well, we can retrace the hoofprints to the Bar M and try them on the horse for size. If that's not enough, we have you. Another Freis flunky. No telling what'll pop out if we squeeze you hard enough." Margot turned to McManus then, and Ki sensed she was having a good time dishing it out, making him squirm. "Purdue and the horse, smack to your gate. Who else wants to stop the Emerald? Who's got better reason than you to kill my jacks and blow up my dam?"

"None of my crew would murder, at least not on my orders," McManus gasped hoarsely. "Don't you dare spread false accusations."

"I can back up what I say. Can you?"

Stung, he stared at her. And Ki, watching, realized Margot had managed to stab McManus at the core of his overweaning pride. McManus, as if reading the truth in Margot's steadfast face, swung his resentment on Grosner. "Where's Justin? Talk up!"

"Go hump yourself. I ain't nobody's nursemaid."

Now insult was added, and McManus stiffened. "You will not scorn me, Rube. You will talk to me." In a fell swoop, he plucked his pistol from his holster. McManus acted so swiftly and impulsively that he was poking the gun into Grosner's belly before anybody reacted, his emotions kindling his voice, making it bearish. "And you will talk respectfully!"

"Put that gun back down," Margot snapped.

McManus impatiently shook his head and launched into a tirade at Grosner. "From the start of my fight with Emerald, you and Justin have tried goading me into what

I should do, and Vincent Freis has tried ordering what I must do. Now, I want to hear from your own lips, Rube, the full story of what's going on behind my back. And don't think you're not going to do it."

McManus won the first round, if only because Grosner was disarmed. The contemptuous smirk skewed into a hapless grin. "You wouldn't shoot a feller, would you? Hey, guys, he's got a gun."

Nobody moved. The Bar M crew disliked Grosner almost as much as they did Purdue, so even if they hadn't been under the weapons of Emerald's jacks, they wouldn't have helped him pull free of their own boss. Margot and the jacks knew Grosner to be a flunky of the despised marshal, and they were enjoying this too much to interfere. Grosner remained in the grip of the wrathfully affronted rancher.

"Yeah, and I want to hear what you know about this rigger's killing that's being laid in my lap, tarnishing my reputation. But I'm not hearing much," McManus growled menacingly. "Okay, Rube, maybe Henri will have better luck loosing your rusty tongue."

Stark terror caught Grosner's features, the threat of Henri more terrifying than of being shot. "You can't! Ain't fair!"

"One way or another, Rube, I'm going to hear how possibly the rigger ties in with my lawsuit, before folks start hearing and thinking dishonest and poorly of me. Same goes for Justin." McManus glanced at Margot. "Even if I've got to drag him out of the marshal's office, I'm going to roust up Purdue and have us a reckoning. I—"

Grosner lunged, ramming against McManus, grasping the pistol, and deflecting it in case McManus should squeeze the trigger. With his other hand he twisted the squirming rancher to shield himself. In the final second of wrenching the pistol away, Grosner caught his own finger in the trigger guard and accidentally laced a shot through the crown of McManus' hat—not that he cared.

McManus did, his face splotching crimson from the feel of the bullet channeling through his hair. Sick with the realization of his own stupidity, McManus tried to wheel around and wrestle his pistol back again, but Grosner had him in a painful lock, and he couldn't do much more than wriggle ineffectually.

"Settle down, or my next one'll clean your ears," Grosner snarled; then he snapped out at the others, "You know who'll get it if anyone tries anything. It won't be me." He lugged McManus with him to his horse, snagged a rein, and led them both back into the woods. "Don't nobody move or try to follow!"

They vanished into the blackness of the timber. The sound of Grosner's getaway was broken by McManus' blistering curses as he came plodding out.

A couple of the Bar M crew made as if to mount and pursue, responding more out of instinct than sense, their weapons still on the ground. "Not worth the risk," Ki advised them. "Grosner would hear you coming and pick you off in the dark."

Margot couldn't help smiling at McManus' come-down, her voice lightly mocking. "And you think you know so much about things. You have a pair of murdering thugs running loose around your ranch. You keep company with their shyster of a boss."

McManus shrugged morosely and then straightened his shoulders. "Okay, I've earned some lumps. But I swear, the Bar M was no more a party to your worker's death than we were to your husband's."

"But you were invading Emerald property and wrecking our dam. You and your hands are guilty as sin."

"I see." McManus's eyes brightened. "Now come the terms."

Margot made a dismissive gesture with her hand. "I don't intend to hold this against you—unless, of course, you try something like it again. I believe it is you who haven't given me a fair shake. There're as many different types of loggers as there are ranchers, and your prejudices about us strike me as hooey. There're ways for both cows and lumber to coexist around here, and all it takes is cooperation, but as long as we don't have any, I plan on trouncing you in court and harvesting my sections, and the Bar M can go suck eggs. And I refuse to talk about a truce with you, Mr. McManus, as long as you're cozy with Freis. Now, get out, the lot of you."

His face flush from her lecture, McManus made no response as he and his crew mounted up and started away. Ledbetter looked around and then asked, "Where's Fong? He was just here."

"I don't know and don't care," McManus grouchily answered, pushing on. "The rascal probably split for the trees, fearing he was going to be the one to take all the heat, him having done it."

Less than three yards from where the crew had mounted, Ki hunkered in some brush and grinned as he overheard them. When minutes before it had seemed to him that matters were winding up, he had quietly drifted away and hid from the group to avoid having to explain why he was staying instead of leaving. Now, as the drumming of hoofbeats died in the night, he saw Margot and the jacks heading off toward whatever forest trail had led them here.

"I got your message," Ki told Margot, when he caught up.

Margot smiled. "Well, if there was anything you'd have remembered us by, we figured it'd be a noose—with space to stick your neck through when you planted your charges. Oh, and thanks for your note."

Bjorn nodded. "I find it wane changing."

"But why'd you hold off and have me blow the dam?"

"Some had other ideas, but the lady here swings a mean axe," Aubrecht quipped. It prompted a ripple of laughter, an amiable show of the affection and loyalty the jacks had for their boss. Aubrecht continued, "And if her idea backfired, we planned to use our ideas: burning the ranch down, torching the summer hay, killing the herd to the last calf. Was lucky that you didn't wipe out the dam completely."

Another jack, apparently one of the construction crew, then explained to Ki, "What blew had to go anyhow. It was to be part of a midspan, but with the other end unbuilt, it was loosening and leaning, and hell, we were setting to blast it next week."

"But after reading your note, Ki, I figured McManus might as well save us the cost and get caught doing it," Margot added serenely. "He won't dream of raiding Emerald again, and I think he's coming around to see Freis for what he is, even to break with him. I chalk this night up as a success."

"We may need more like tonight," Ki said, rubbing an earlobe. "We haven't pulled all of Freis' fangs."

★

Chapter 13

All during the dam escapade and on through the night, Jessie and Duncan rode a troubled trail. The day ahead would be brutal and deadly, so they tried to gain crucial rest by taking turns fitfully napping in the saddle. Sleep was elusive. They struggled to determine their bearings while blazing a course through the black swale of rocks and forests. Frequently they struck matches to review Duncan's map, and almost as often they wound up lost or boxed, and had to retrace their steps. Yet they kept pressing onward, goaded by urgency, in the direction they hoped would bring them to Wapato Gorge.

Late, very late, Jessie awoke from a short, nodding doze in the saddle. Darkness still clung to the cracks and crevices, but now the moon was fading, and a faint luminous band was seeping along the eastern sky. They pushed higher into the rugged, timbered hills while the horizon grew brassy. The dawning sun found them reaching a local summit where they could look out over a wild expanse of rocks, woods, and a gorge that cut through the ridges.

After dismounting, they walked through an intervening hedge of low shrubbery to a ledge and eyed the precipitous drop into the gorge. The sides were steep, mostly bare, and showed the erosive scars left by a river that had once gouged its passage ages ago. The gorge floor was now a fertile trough of tall grasses, bushy thickets, and conifer and hardwood groves. To the left they heard the rush of water, although no stream was visible.

Far to the left, however, Jessie was able to glimpse the roof of a small structure. It appeared to be in the crook of stony outcrop where it would command a view of the gorge and the rim.

"If that's the shanty," Duncan remarked skeptically, when Jessie pointed it out, "the prospector must've been nuts. But then, most of 'em are, and it does make a helluva lookout post against robbers sneaking up. Or us, come to consider. It's worth a try."

After returning to their horses, they headed left and pretty soon hit a faint trail that flanked the rim. It was a path first laid out by animals, Jessie surmised as they followed it, and it probably led to water or a source of food. Since the water heard earlier was becoming louder, she guessed the former.

"Shanty or no, one thing's certain," Duncan said, as they entered a hollow. "Thurlow could've trekked those gorge walls afoot, but Paw had a gimp and couldn't. No horse could, either."

The hollow grew thick with brush and stunted trees. Windswept limbs were twisted at every conceivable angle. The clutter was greatest on their side of a stream, which meandered across their path and brought them to a halt. It was not wide or deep, but it flowed surging by and over the rim of the gorge. Its splashing cascade, Jessie realized, caused the noise they'd heard.

The other side of the clearing had some growth, but

mostly it was a grassy glen that stretched open to the gorge. The ashes of a few bygone campfires were dotted about, and two well-trodden paths intersected near the middle. One trail headed on parallel with the gorge. The other came in from upstream, crossed the first, and went out by way of a scooped niche in the rim, where it evidently made a stab at descending to the gorge.

Just before they started to ford the stream, they spotted someone cresting that impossible trail, and they faded back into the brush. The floppy slouch hat they first spied rose to include a bewhiskered old trapper, who was panting with exhaustion as he climbed to the ledge leading a small burro and carrying a bundle of wolf traps over his shoulder. When he got to where the trails met, he angled to the stream and squatted for a long drink.

Duncan whispered to Jessie, "I don't like the smell of this. Maybe the codger is what he seems to be, but I don't want to risk it."

"Chances are he's been setting traps in the gorge and has worked his way up here to do the same," Jessie replied. "If that's all, we can afford to wait until he's done. If not . . . " She shrugged.

For the space of an hour, they sat watching the trapper place traps along the stream and around the camping area. Not once did he act out of character that Jessie could see, and after all, this was a watering place for all manner of wildlife and, therefore, a choice spot for trappers to work. Finally he got his burro from where he'd left it by the stream and hiked off upstream along the trail.

They waited a few more minutes, then dashed across the stream, and rode away from the glen on the trail that skirted the gorge. For another half hour they traveled at a cautious gait until they finally rounded the curve of the outcrop and sighted what they hoped was the prospector's shanty. Immediately they veered into the concealment of a trailside pocket, where they reined up and dismounted.

After conferring for a moment, they climbed and carefully circled above the shanty on the ridge of the outcrop. Then they eased down directly toward the shanty, sitting, digging bootheels into the steep slope to avoid dislodging a pebble or stream of dirt that would betray them. They hadn't spotted any horse, and the structure appeared deserted.

After wriggling through a rhododendron jungle, which grew up to the rear wall of the shanty, they straightened to peer through a narrow opening that had once been a window. The short, square interior was murky, but enough sunlight filtered in to reveal Rachel lying on the hard rock floor, her wrists and ankles trussed with rawhide strings, her mouth gagged with an old neckerchief. Rachel started nervously when Duncan tapped the window ledge with his fingernails, but then her eyes sparked with relief, and she nodded eagerly when he mouthed to find out if she was alone.

Dipping, Jessie and Duncan wormed through more flowers and ducked along the side to the front wall of the shanty. They saw nobody, but still fearing a trap, Jessie stayed crouched with her revolver in hand, while Duncan sprang across and through the door. Pausing only long enough to cut the strings, he half carried, half dragged his niece out of the shanty, supporting her shaky limbs while he sped headlong for the pocket, Jessie a pace behind.

Once back with the horses, Duncan stripped off her gag and Rachel gasped breathlessly, "Where am I? How'd I get here?"

"Wapato Gorge, gal. Can't you remember what happened?"

"I remember calling you, then nothing till I found myself tied up and all alone in there." Wincing, she fingered the welt on her head. "Well, no wonder. I must've been knocked unconscious."

"You were," Jessie said, giving Rachel her canteen. "You were kidnapped and were being held here for ransom by one of the raiders."

"Freis," Duncan stated flatly. "I dunno why he left you alone, maybe 'cause he had to show for law duty, but it weren't from cold feet. He'll come any time after the beaver skins, so we'd better go. Are you steady enough to ride back double with me?"

"I've had more sleep and rest than I care for. My hands and feet are a bit numb, and I'm hungry, that's all. But ride back where, Uncle Dunc? Our cabin? Uh-uh, it won't be any safer there than it was last night. We might as well stay here." Rachel paused thoughtfully, then returned the canteen to Jessie with thanks. "Why not? Isn't Wapato Gorge where Grandad was talking about before he died?"

"Yeah, and I can't deny I ain't curious," Duncan allowed. "'Cept he was out of his mind, don't forget, and snooping around at the bottom could take time, and we didn't bring any bedrolls."

Rachel humphed. "I'm quite prepared to sleep on the ground. It's a practice I've become accustomed to traveling with you." She turned to Jessie. "Is that all right with you?"

"Oh, yes. I've a hunch it'd be interesting to look."

"I suppose if the cabin is out," Duncan said, sighing, "goin' down there can't do us worse than goin' anyplace else for the now."

With Rachel riding tandem with Duncan, the trio headed back along the trail to the glen, which was the only spot where they'd seen any sign of a pathway down or a break in the gorge's cliffside. When they arrived and took a close gander at the path, though, they realized their horses would never make it. Duncan even questioned how the trapper's sure-footed burro had managed not to fall. They picketed their mounts out to graze, Jessie and Duncan reluctantly leaving their rifles behind as well. But they did bring the beef jerky, parched corn, and chocolate bars that they'd packed in their saddlebags. They started their descent.

The path was akin to a portage trail that had been traveled by Indians and explorers for a hundred years before the arrival of settlers. Notched and slashed along the eighty-degree cliff, sometimes dogging segments of natural ledges, it led to the bottom in a zigzag of switchbacks, with only projecting roots of scrub giving occasional holds. Then three-quarters down, it became a more torturous route, scarcely a path at all. A mere series of holds connected by stone juttings in the deeply scalloped wall.

For what seemed an eternity, the three stalked their slow and cautious way down, anxiously aware that any misstep could spill them to their death. Eventually the acute rake of the cliff curved outward to form an angled bank of boulders and small timber. To their right, now, they saw a stream fed by a pool worn into the bedrock, and the pool, in turn, was supplied by the waterfall tumbling hundreds of feet from the lip of the gorge. Instead of staying on the right, the stream slewed toward them, virtually disappeared as it tunneled underneath a broad arch of slabstone and rubbled slag, then resurfaced to their left, where it churned merrily on. The path became comparatively easy after it crossed the malformed bridge and at last deposited them in the foliage-choked pit of the gorge.

At first they went to the right, hiking through cottonwoods and elders and thickets of creepers. Gradually fir and pine and grape grew more prevalent, along with boulders and stone depressions deep in shadow. It took Jessie awhile to realize this pattern of vegetation was because of comparative dryness, due to the stream's flowing the other way. It dawned on her what it all might mean.

"Listen," she said, calling a halt, "Thurlow was hunting beaver, and beaver live around water. We're heading the wrong way."

"Every way could be the wrong way," Duncan countered, but he didn't argue as they retraced their steps to the path.

Now they began to follow the stream more or less. They clambered over house-size rocks, fought through morasses of berry vines and bushes, squeezed past tight swaths of maples and beech—not sticking to any path, but merely believing that terrain like this usually meant beaver, and where there was beaver, there may have been Thurlow. Sometimes the stream bubbled and stewed in moss-fringed channels. Other times it would widen into placid ponds ringed by alder, honeysuckle, and birch, or spread wider still into marshes profuse with cattails and skunk cabbage.

The air was vibrant with little scuttlings, tiny chirps, and buzzings. Sparrows took wing from branches of aspen and elder. Toads splashed in the stagnant waters, snagging meals from clouds of gnats and mosquitoes. Dank, aromatic odors wafted from the leaf mold underfoot, its softness silencing the tread of boots.

The stream made a bend, a sward of grass and saplings thriving in its curve. And it was then, while rounding the bend, that they came face to face with a grisly sight. A human skeleton lay on a level patch of weeds beside the water. Its legs were still encased in boots, the leather of which showed the gnaw marks of wild animals' fangs. Months of weathering and the ravages of predatory beasts had left the bones clean and white. The skull was missing.

Rachel initially glimpsed the skull, a glint of white out in the water attracting her eye. With a shuddery gasp, she pointed it out to Jessie and Duncan, and now they all saw the head leering up through the stream, teeth exposed in a haunting grin, the hollow eye sockets regarding them gruesomely.

Her boots sinking into mud, Jessie reached to recover the human skull. Using a tuft of grass, she wiped the cranium free of encrusted slime, and in doing so, she revealed a black, corroded coin set into the bone just above the left temple.

"Thurlow," Duncan proclaimed, reverently doffing his hat. "Not another head in ten million would carry such a silver dollar."

"Zack said the secret was in Thurlow's brain," Jessie mused. "He meant it literally, of course, since Thurlow would've known the location of his own cache. But I wonder if he wasn't also thinking figuratively, like he was when he called this a 'silver skull'."

Duncan said, "You can't do Thurlow no harm checking over his remains, and Paw had something in mind."

Acting on her hunch, Jessie took out her knife and opened a blade which could be used as an awl. She set to work probing around the coin. The skull proved easy to carve. Prying free the dollar, she gently scraped off corrosion. Yet something else was there, she perceived,

154

and continuing with infinite care, she lightly removed more corrosion, finally exposing a set of tiny, disjointed lines. After pondering to make sense of them, she was able to form nine letters:

UNDER FIRE

Smiling, Jessie looked up and, as she pocketed her knife, chanced to note the sun was already lowering into the trees upon the rim. It came as a surprise to her that they had spent the bulk of a day down at the gorge's bottom. But it was worth it, she thought, crossing to where Duncan was comforting his niece.

"Look here," she said, showing them the marked coin.

Duncan studied it, frowning. "What does it mean?"

"Zack would've known right off. It's not code, just shorthand, and besides, Zack was aware of what Thurlow was doing and about where and only needed the gist of a message."

"So Dad warned he was under attack?" Rachel suggested quizzically.

"Well, Thurlow probably wrote it, assuming he had a sharp blade and the time, which he wouldn't have if attacked. Or Zack scratched it for reasons I can't figure, and he was too delirious to tell it to me straight." Jessie shrugged. "We're liable never to learn all the details, but we can basically conclude it was an arrangement between them in case of accidents or, well, what did happen. Nobody but close kin would think to look under his hair."

"Great," Duncan said testily, "now, what does it mean?"

"It could refer to his main campfire, his home base."

"How many hundred campfires have there been hereabouts? Old, new, you can't tell 'em apart after two days of cold ashes. We've no idea where his main camp was."

"I do, folks." At the same instant the gravelly voice barked behind them, they heard the oily click of a gun being cocked. Wheeling too late to draw, they stared at the man stepping out from hiding, sunlight winking off his leveled revolver. The man was a tall, hard-muscled stranger with a mashed red nose.

"Who're you?" Duncan demanded. "You with Freis?"

"Justin Purdue," the man said, smirking maliciously. "Freis ain't joinin' this party. No need to, I know where the camp's at."

"From when you killed Dad?" Rachel lashed out, voice taut with grief.

Purdue drawled sadistically, "Yeah, sweetie. Your fool kin bragged about the stash, and Freis picked me as pard 'cause I've lived 'round the Rogue since ten and know it blind." Carefully he yanked Duncan's and Jessie's revolvers from their holsters, stuffing them in his belt. "We tracked the camp, but only Thurlow was there, and he got away—for a while, to here, like you." Then he took out a couple of piggin strings. "Here, sweetie, tie their hands like I done yours, and you best do it tight."

Helpless, Rachel proceeded grudgingly to secure her uncle and Jessie with the rawhide thongs, while Purdue watched smugly and boasted, "Yeah, like I been tracking y'all, outflanking you stumblebums at every turn. Figured you might lead me to the skins. All of 'em, not some handout I'd gotten if I'd waited for you to pay off." Seeing Rachel was finished, he warily holstered his revolver just long enough to knot her wrists together again. "Okay, start walkin' that way. One booger move, and I'll shoot y'all."

During their passage through the gorge's woodland, Purdue played it sure and safe, stalking at their backs

156

and keeping his gun unwaveringly trained. "What're you so gloomy about?" he jeered. "Sweetie's returned to the fold, so now I'm due my price."

"While double-crossing your boss?" Duncan retorted.

"Hell, just collecting back wages. Saw my chance and grabbed it by grabbing her, Freis bein' too broke and in a jam to pay me."

"I thought he's too smart to get in trouble," Jessie prompted.

"So did he. But he's too greedy, is all, selling land Grand Americana has under lease just to gyp McManus with a fat mortgage. When McManus sued Emerald, Freis realized a trial would expose him, same's probate would if he tried covering up by busting off McManus."

"He decided to bust Emerald instead," Jessie suggested. "Bust Emerald with dirty tricks like busting off Eliot Gideon."

"Yeah, and I didn't get paid for that or for yesterday's job," Purdue complained, as much to himself as anyone. "I'm fed up with workin' for free. And did double shifts. First, raid you; then check on Bar M's blastin' Emerald's dam. I made my own plans now, I did."

Jessie felt her heart quickening at his reference to the explosive attack, and then her heart began pounding her ribs as she heard Purdue continue griping, "Oh sure, Freis keeps promising money'll be coming. And yeah, he's expecting Great Americana to be sending up a huge wad of it any day now. It's overdue, in fact, but that dope ain't in no hurry to receive it."

"Nice of Grand Americana to bail out Freis," Jessie remarked blithely, checking her rising emotions. "But can he buy his way clear? It'd get him off the hook, but McManus doesn't want to sell, and the real owner of the land doesn't, either."

"The cash ain't to help Freis personally," Purdue replied, too preoccupied with his grouching to notice how much Jessie seemed to know. "Grand Americana has it pegged for property deals, part of some notion to take over most around here. And I know for a fact that Americana warned him to straighten out his mess by time it arrives." Purdue gave a grating laugh. "Naw, Freis needs dough to rent gents like me. Course, he's got Americana connections and influence, so he probably promises he'll hire the small army he can raise overnight if need be. He's coming to that, fast, and I hope he does. 'Cause when the dust settles, he'll still have his mess and no money, and I'll be able to just slide right into his empty boots."

Jessie drew a deep breath, her pulse throbbing violently as she considered this maze of crossed purposes and conflicting motives. She surmised that through Grand Americana, the cartel probably aimed to gain control of the Rogue River Valley, the only suitable area in Oregon for traversing the Siskiyous. The loot she'd retrieved from Pritt was to help fund this scheme and was to be delivered here to Freis in his capacity as Americana lawyer. Once having a stranglehold on the passage, the cartel would be able to check the nation's development, the sort of squeeze play they relished.

Yet Freis proved so crooked that the cartel was squeezing him as well to undo his private swindle. Needing money to retain gunmen, he'd strongarmed Thurlow, and failing that, had bided his time. Time was up, he'd reckoned, when he learned that Duncan and Rachel were en route, and he'd made a furious try to torture the secret out of Zack. He'd taken Bruno because Purdue was busy at the Bar M. Freis had used Bar M's lawsuit as excuse

158

and his fake mortgage as leverage to demand McManus protect his interests by accepting Purdue and Grosner, who were thus positioned perfectly to raid and kill, the blame falling on the Bar M. Obviously Freis' plan was to foment such a feud that Emerald would be driven broke and the Bar M would be so drained that he could foreclose his phony mortgage, thereby recovering the land. Nobody would be the wiser.

And it was working. Bar M's being goaded into blowing up Emerald's dam was evidence of that. If it didn't work, if Freis felt he no longer could afford to pussyfoot, then he could form a gang in short order and destroy Emerald.

She could not stop Freis. Jessie was under no illusions as to what Purdue would do once the beaver cache was in his possession. She knew the renegade gunman intended to kill them in cold blood, even as he had killed Gideon and the rigger, and she felt there was scant hope of surviving, most of it resting on her hidden derringer.

"That's it," Purdue announced, as they entered a clearing.

The camp, what was left of it, lay in neat ruin—a contradiction that didn't make immediate sense to Jessie, disbelieving Freis or Purdue would clean up after ransacking Thurlow's belongings. Yet at the edge of the otherwise bare glade were tattered remnants, the broken frame of a stretch rack, and a rusty spade and other discarded tools and effects. Then, detecting scuffed bootprints and regarding the heap of the campfire, she realized subsequent campers had picked up the litter, desiring to stay here. Indeed, it was choicely situated on a level rise, protected by boulders and a copse of alders with a bubbling spring only paces away. And now, twilight's lavender shadows were tinging the glade with beauty. It was hard for Jessie to conceive that this campground was to become her graveyard.

"All right," Purdue snapped at Duncan, "I heard the talking, so no use trying to bluff me. You know where the skins are. Show me."

Duncan shook his head. "Paw and my brother didn't cave in, even when tortured. I'll see you in hell afore I betray them."

"Think so, eh?" Purdue cocked his revolver and thrust its muzzle against Rachel's temple. "You ain't keeping your end of our bargain, so I'll just take back mine," he rasped, needled by impatience. "Five seconds, pal, then five more for your friend."

Jessie saw the frustrated anguish in Duncan's eyes and read that he still had not fathomed the location of the cache. With desperation she cried hoarsely, "Don't shoot." She seemed to wilt. "You win, Purdue."

Duncan looked stricken. "Jessie!"

"No use us all dying." Defiance ebbed from her eyes. "I-I know where the pelts are. Untie me, and I'll unbury them for you."

"Later," Purdue sneered, grinning with triumph. "I ain't loosening nobody's hands till I get mine on 'em. Okay, you show me."

Jessie, losing her bid to get free and at her derringer, shrugged in apparent hopelessness and trudged across to the old campfire. She pointed to the ashes with the toe of her boot. "Under there."

Purdue circled the campfire and faced her. "That's dumb."

Jessie shook her head, her voice dead. "Pelts store forever as long as they're dry. Keeping them in waterproofing and building a fire to dispell any ground moisture is a smart way to stash them."

Watching Jessie carefully, Purdue holstered his revolver and knelt, digging his hands tentatively into the soft ashes and clearing aside the charred wood. Then he paused and looked across at Jessie, skepticism narrowing his greedy eyes. "Don't you be tricking me."

"The stash is under the fire. You have to go deeper."

Purdue began to lean forward, grunted, then straightened to lay the revolvers close to one side. "That's better," he muttered, crouching to tear into the ashes, pawing, scooping a hole down into the dirt. It was soft under the ashes, proof that the hard earth had been excavated here and then refilled, and it made Purdue feverish with haste. He began digging faster, alternating his cupped hands as he sent dirt and ashes flying.

Abruptly something seemed to explode from the ground, throwing dust and charcoal into Purdue's hand. With a shriek of agony, he reared back—to reveal his left hand locked in a wolf trap that had been buried under the campfire.

Jessie sprang like a panther, diving to snatch her revolver with her trussed hands. Purdue lunged to block her, only to be wrenched back by a strong steel cable which connected the trap to a peg buried in the earth. More blood spurted from his fingers. Jessie punted her revolver a few feet and followed to make another scoop at it, managing to fumble it between her palms and then groping frantically to clasp it effectively. Bellowing, Purdue jerked his right hand to his holster, snapping up his pistol and thumbing back the hammer.

Jessie squeezed the trigger. The recoil in her awkward hand jarred her back a pace as the bullet slanted down

161

and smashed through the lapel of Purdue's shirt, drilling his left lung. His slug whined past Jessie's ear and off into space. Lashing out a boot, she kicked the smoking pistol from Purdue's grasp, then pivoted and kicked Duncan's Starr .44 away from Purdue's temptation.

Purdue remained on his knees, his face pallid, blood welling through the fabric of his shirt. "P-please, pry me loose."

"Later," Jessie retorted, crossing to Duncan and Rachel. No one could show more pity than she when pity was due, and no one could give less when it was not merited.

All but fainting with pain, Purdue watched dazedly while his three ex-prisoners plucked deftly at one another's ties, his mind seeming unable to absorb his fate. "How . . . How'd you . . . ?"

"I didn't know it," Jessie answered, feeling slack in her knotted thong. "This morning we watched a trapper set traps under several campfires, a favorite spot, because animals like to paw into garbage, hunting bones and so forth. That's why I wanted you to dig the fire. This is a popular campsite, and I hoped, prayed, that the trapper or some other had stopped through here."

"The, the skins . . . You were faking me all along, gal?"

To Purdue's surprise, Jessie shook her head. Her wrists free, she went and picked up Thurlow's rusty spade and then took it to the campfire and started shoveling next to where the trap had been laid. Two feet under the surface, the spade struck an oilcloth bundle. The pouched neck of the oilcloth had been tied and folded and tied again. It took Jessie a few minutes to unwrap it, and when she opened the oilcloth, she had to remove the board that was levering down flat the contents underneath.

"Beaver pelts," Jessie declared. Peeling off the uppermost one, she rose to display it. "There's a fortune of them down there, all right, unless beaverskin hats suddenly go out of vogue."

She hesitated, seeing that Purdue had fallen forward across the wolf trap while she had been excavating the cache. She doubted if the gunman had witnessed her victory, for Justin Purdue was dead.

Chapter 14

Ki did not sleep on the office sofa that night.

He drowsed in a brass bed. The curtains were pulled, but a candle was left aglow, allowing him to see as well as feel Margot's warm body stretching alongside him. He also heard her—Margot in a chatty mood, asking innocuous questions and then prattling on.

"I went to school, too. Got through my seventh reader, Ki, but from there I was on my own. Met Eliot while I was tending tables in a café this timber company crew liked going to. He'd gone to college and could compute more timber in five minutes than the boss logger could figure in a season. Do you mind me talking?"

"No," Ki murmured. It was true; he knew she needed an outlet.

"I'll shut up. Eliot always chided me for babbling afterward."

Shifting, Ki stroked her cheek affectionately to confirm it was all right, but that only seemed to make her shut up. For a half dozen seconds they looked in each other's eyes; then his fingers wandered from her cheek to one breast, teasing her nipple erect; then they glided down across her smooth belly to the soft, pulsing warmth below.

She moaned, her flesh alive to his caresses, and her voice sighed in his ear. "Make it as good as last time."

He kissed her mouth and the nape of her neck; the breast with its engorged nipple he suckled between his lips. Margot responded fiercely, squirming against him, draping one bent leg over him in an effort to thrust closer, then hesitating, withdrawing her swollen breast.

"My turn this time," she whispered, curling to return his kisses, her tongue darting across his tiny nipples . . . swirling lower along his taut abdomen . . . then still lower, probing and exploring the fleshy shaft of his erection, finally plunging her mouth voraciously over it, swallowing him in a softly clinging pressure.

Ki felt his hips writhing, stirring with sensations, a hungry vacuum drawing all his vital juices to his groin. And Margot seemed to be enjoying this almost as much as he, clawing at his buttocks, her tongue licking and twining, her teeth gently nipping, her lips firmly stroking, impatiently greedy to savor the tumultuous eruption building in him.

But surprising Ki, she pulled away just as he was verging on climax. Pivoting up, she straddled him with her knees on either side of his hips, her eyes gazing down at him full of passion. Then with one hand to help guide him, she impaled herself on his spearing hardness, contracting her strong hips so that the muscular action squeezed her passage tightly around his girth.

Ki clenched his buttocks, thrusting his pelvis. Margot spread her thighs, so that, sliding up and down, she soon contained the whole of him in her. Together they struck a pumping rhythm that pleased them both, Ki fondling her jiggling breasts, Margot arching to reach back down

166

behind and massage Ki's scrotum. It didn't take long for the erotic sensations surging within their bodies to become unbearable and then to burst, Ki erupting far up into her while her face contorted and twisted in orgasm.

With the ebbing of passion, Margot crouched limply over Ki. Slowly she eased off his body and contentedly cradled in his arms. They dozed, remaining firmly embraced . . .

Ki awoke sometime later. It was still dark, but he didn't know the time and really didn't care. He lay quietly listening to Margot's heavy breathing. He hadn't been awakened by intuition, by some premonition of impending doom; he simply had to take a leak. The chamberpot was wedged too far under the bed to grab without disturbing Margot. So carefully easing from Margot, who rolled mumbling in her sleep, Ki quietly dressed and tiptoed outside to the nearby outhouse.

Stepping from the outhouse to return, however, Ki abruptly flattened against its door and stood stock still. A shadow drifted by him. Clouds had formed since last night's clear sky, and in the moonless gloom of this early morning hour, he could see merely the silhouette of a body under a Stetson. But that hat was a sufficient tip for Ki.

Ki began stalking the stranger, curious as to his purpose, and presently saw him halt and lie prone in the cover bush about five feet from Margot's bungalow. Ki sucked in his breath and was padding to within a few yards of the man when the man suddenly straightened and moved forward, stooping under her window. A match flared, and Ki caught a brief glimpse of the man's face. It was Rube Grosner. Something started to hiss and sputter. A black powder cartridge! Grosner was lighting its fuse.

Instantly Ki launched himself upward and out. He landed on Grosner's back, and there came a startled curse as Ki, chopping down with the edge of his palm, felt Grosner go limp. The fuse was sputtering merrily. Frantically Ki ground it out beneath his heel.

In that moment of anxiety, Ki was intent solely on the fuse. Then he was aware of a running figure—Grosner, who'd merely been stunned, had come out of it and was fleeing for the trees. As Ki wheeled, gunfire flamed from the darkness, and a slug droned past his hip. He loosed a *shuriken* and Grosner toppled end over end.

He saw another figure vaulting from the near bunkhouse, pistol held high. He shouted, not wishing to be mistaken for an enemy and shot. It was Aubrecht who answered him, yelling, "Che-rist, what's cooking? That you, Ki?"

Ki called in response. There came from the bunkhouse loud turmoil and cries, the jacks boiling outside in a rush. Ki went to Grosner and found him dead, the *shuriken* having slashed his throat and severed both jugulars. He was dragging Grosner by a foot from the great puddle of blood when he was joined by Aubrecht and Bjorn.

Aubrecht grinned at Ki. "Should've done this last night, taken 'em first." He pawed in Grosner's pockets and brought out a cartridge and more fuse. "Well, now we know what dirty raw job he was sent here to do."

"Already has done," Ki corrected dryly, showing the stick and fuse he'd snuffed out by the bungalow. And with the rest of the jacks and Margot now gathering around, he recounted what had occurred.

A council of war then developed, one of the jacks declaring harshly, "The dam wasn't enough! The bar M's at it again."

168

"It must be," Margot agreed. "I'm sorry; I was wrong."

"Ain't your fault, Boss," another jack said. "We all thunk they'd learn their lesson, but bein' soft on 'em was a mistake."

"Only thing to do now is take the play away from them," Gerry Shaw stated. "Strike them hard, fast; burn every stick down."

Ki, remaining quiet while more threats of retaliation were voiced and approved, finally spoke up. "I think we'd better stay put and set up a strong defense."

"What d'you mean?"

"Well, look, it doesn't make much sense for Grosner to have snuck in here, just to blow up Margot. McManus isn't so stupid to believe such an act would force Emerald to cave in to him, right?"

Aubrecht snapped his fingers. "No reason not to hit back."

"Yes, for two reasons. Suppose this wasn't Bar M's doing, but was to make us think so and hit back. Sure, Grosner's virtually a crewman there, but we also know he stooges for Freis. And I happen to know the Bar M doesn't have any cartridges like these. Or suppose this was to be a signal. McManus or Freis may well have a gang not far from here, ready to bust in here once they hear the explosions and to clean us out in our confusion."

"Good suspicionin'," a jack said. "I'll buy it's a raid."

"They'd likely attack signal or no," Margot allowed, sighing heavily. "You're right, Ki; we'll hole in. What else can we do?"

Ki smiled encouragingly. "We could, like Gerry said, take the play away from them. They figure on surprising us, but now we can surprise them. Catch them in a sweet ambush surprise."

Gerry asked, "Yeah, but what if the mistake is yours?"

"Okay, assume I'm wrong, and no gang is out there preparing to storm us. We've rigged a trap for nothing, but lost nothing but sleep."

"Let's split up, half here and there," Maxwell suggested, then slapped his thigh. "Hell'n spittin' devils, this'll be fun."

Soon ten riders were galloping out of camp, and what they might have lacked in numbers, they made up for in toughness and resolve. Staying behind with instructions where to send a messenger in case of a flanking sneak attack were the remaining nine jacks, posted in strategic points, and Cookie, who elected to stick close by the bungalow as a defender of it and Margot.

The spot chosen for ambush was roughly a half mile out along the wagon trail leading to the main road. Ki and the jacks spread out across the sides of a short draw, one of the few places near the camp that afforded height and field of vision with the cover of shouldering woods. In addition to his hand weapons, Ki was armed with a borrowed rifle—an old but well-kept .403.

Five minutes later, someone in the camp touched off the two sticks Grosner had been carrying. Everybody was anticipating the blasts, yet the sticks detonated with such brilliant force, that all along the draw, men jerked behind their shelter. Then, as the noise and fire echoed across the forests, they settled to await events.

Crouching, Ki wondered if his theory would pan out. There'd been no sign of gunmen close by the camp, but he doubted that Freis—and he was convinced it would be Freis, not McManus—would plan his assault that way. It would be too risky for a gang to weasel through the timber and surround the camp undetected, whereas one man could sneak in and out, his explosive sabotage sowing panic, killing the boss, and signaling the gang.

170

Speed, not stealth, would now be most important, and the raiders would charge via the fastest route, along the wagon road. That is, if Ki were correct in his figuring.

Once, faint and far, Ki thought he heard horses. Rising, he cast a look in the direction of the camp, fearing the gang had cut around behind them. But no sounds, no gunfire, came from there. And ahead was deserted. Was he wrong?

Then, suddenly, he perceived the approach of a rhythmic pounding...a ground-drumming roll that quickly sharpened into the thunder of hooves.

With the jacks, Ki focused on the far sweep of the draw, just as the first push of riders careened around a bend and entered it. Behind streamed more, a looming flow of big men on big horses. Thirty, Ki estimated, maybe more—the size of the gang stunning him, for it was much larger than the Bar M crew and many times more than the motley bunch working for Freis.

They drove toward the camp at a headlong clip, nothing in their manner indicating they expected an ambush. Ki searched their midst but couldn't spot Purdue, but, yes, there was Freis looking plump with confidence. It was evident that he'd somehow managed to collect a horde in one day, taking personal command to ensure success. Freis must have reckoned, and rightly so, that the vastly outnumbered jacks would be hard pressed to defend their camp, much less mount a counterattack.

Consequently, Freis and his gang rode with a free rein. The trail blurred under their horses as they came abreast of the jacks, who were far from asleep, but not as awake as they should have been, either.

In that instant, the air cracked from the ripping gunfire pouring in from both sides. The staccato volley emptied three saddles and sent the others flinging for cover, each

171

man for himself as they fanned out while answering with pistol and carbine. The steady exchange of bullets was punctuated with shouts and oaths and howls, and with Freis, his face dark, yelling orders.

The gunmen, stooping low, began charging toward the boulders where the jacks were holed. One man somersaulted backward; two more vaulted his sprawling body, only to be downed in turn. Yet the jacks were in a desperate bind, Ki realized. They had surprised the gang and accounted for eight or nine casualties without receiving a wound. But the odds were still greatly against them, and now that the gunmen had also reached cover, it would only be a matter of time before the ten of them were whittled to zero.

"Hold 'em, boys!" Aubrecht roared. "Hold 'em!"

The gunmen were coming. Urged on by their boss, they were swarming up through the rocks and trees, turning the trail and the shouldering draw into an inferno of blazing gunfire. Twice the jacks held them and sent them recoiling down. Twice the gunmen managed to rally and surge higher, blasting at the thin line of grim defenders. The battle became a melee of pistols and knives and hand-to-hand struggles. The jacks fought like demons, but they could not stem the tide rolling over them.

An attacker, his pistol shot out of his hand, came at Ki with a hefty knife. He got to within a foot, slashing his heavy blade. Then, abruptly, his face went blank; between his eyes appeared a throwing dagger, sunk to its hilt in his brain. Ki retrieved his dagger and, constantly on the outlook for Freis, crossed to the vantage of a large patch of brush—out of which, unnoticed, a gunman arose, a revolver in his fist.

At that moment, Ki glimpsed Freis and drew a bead with his rifle. Then a man dashed between them, and Ki had to hold fire. But the gunnie in the brush did not and triggered. Aubrecht swayed, clasping his arm, his own pistol dropping from nerveless fingers.

Ki, too far away to be of help, swore as he watched Aubrecht fall and more gunmen sweeping forward to engulf two wounded jacks who were still firing next to Aubrecht. Other gunmen, including Freis, were re-mounting to spur their horses along the draw like a charge of cavalry. Only Ki and three jacks remained able enough to stand between them and the Emerald camp.

Hastily reloading, Ki cradled the rifle stock and fired one shot, then loosed a string of them as fast as he could stuff bullets, bolt, and trigger. Reports from the three jacks came even faster, for luckily they were equipped with newer repeating carbines. The riders wavered, two going down and a third slumping.

But it was not enough.

"Fall back to the camp!" Ki shouted. "We'll have to fort there!"

The three jacks, aware they'd die for naught if they stayed and eager to warn those at the camp so a final stand could be made, joined Ki in a scrambling dash for their horses. Then in a mad gallop, the four raced along the wagon road toward the camp, desperate to reach it before the bullets of the pursuing gang found them.

Chapter 15

Ki, Gerry Shaw, Maxwell, and Bjorn.

Behind them the draw appeared choked with raiders, their revolvers and rifles blasting away in erratic though massive volleys. The surviving gunmen, rallied from the ambush and frenzied with bloodlust, attempted by any means to kill the four in front of them, but they couldn't aim effectively from their pitching saddles, and their bullets sailed off—high, low, and wild.

The four in front bent low, knowing their chances of living were remote even if they did make the camp. Shots snapped and whined after them as, finally, they hit the huddled line of buildings. Almost floundering, they veered sharply and sped for whichever door seemed appealingly close, while from the windows blazed covering gunfire.

The gang swerved after them, sending avenging lead sizzling by their heads. Four saddles were emptied by jacks—jacks who were supposed to be unnerved, demoralized by the death of their boss in a bungalow that still was standing. It took a lot of steam out of the gunmen's charge, most of them slowing, pulling rein, none wishing to be a hero.

This slackening allowed the three jacks a momentary

175

reprieve. They dismounted at a run, slapped their horses off, and dived into buildings. Ki plunged up the knoll to the bungalow, hearing a renewed rush to down him before he could reach shelter—only to be stalled again by the guns pouring lead back at them. He sprang from his roan and spanked it to run out of range. He sprinted to the porch just as Margo opened the door and the camp cook reached out to drag him inside.

The door slammed behind him, and despite the murderous barrage, they acknowledged one another, a very brief reunion with surprise and relief and sorrow all tossed together. Then it was over and the seige was on, the camp ravaged by marauding gunmen.

From all directions the defenders responded full blast, lining their shots at the saffron flares that were winking in the darkness outside. Up in the bungalow, Ki worked his .403 rifle from one window, while Margot cannoned an absolute blunderbuss of a shotgun from another. And when Cookie wasn't shooting out the rear, he was distributing boxes of gunshells, having prudently carted up reserve ammunition, along with a supply of his kitchen utensils, while the ambush party had been gone.

A gunman scurrying by Ki abruptly let out a howl and clawed at a hit shoulder. He and another gunman who'd been with him vanished, swearing, into the night. Margot let fly with her shotgun then, and as its thunderous discharge receded, wails and thrashings could be heard from where the men had fled to. In back, Cookie was levering his carbine in rapid fire, muttering as he lambasted dim figures of other advancing men.

The bungalow began to reek with choking fumes, and a fog of smoke thickened down from the ceiling. Lead chewed constantly into the walls and through the windows, zipping and ricocheting. Occasionally above the racket, Ki could hear Freis hurling directions and profanely demanding more action, while his men moved in and about, seeking vulnerable points to strike.

For long hours, the battle raged. Gunmen charged and lumberjack bullets, crying in a steady whine, beat them back. Time and again it appeared as if the three in the bungalow were on the road to hell, as flying wedges of gunmen would breach the porch or rear stoop. And time and again Ki and the cook lay waste of them through the now weak-hinged doorways, while a hellcat widow with eyes glittering like fire dropped men.

And unrelenting throughout was the flow of bullets, spraying from every direction. The old china closet in one corner of the parlor crackled like something afire, the cups, the plates, and the saucers smashing into fragments. But as dawn began to ooze across the eastern horizon, some of the shooting slowly died away. Finally an eerie silence held the camp as a hint of sunrise gilded the sky.

"They got one more stab, I judge," Cookie growled, returning to his post with a bloody bandage around the upper part of his left arm. "Daylight's too risky for the like o' them to stick around. They've got to wipe us out now or pack it in."

"Speak of the devil," Margot snapped. "Here they come."

Straightening, Ki saw that gunmen were bellying up from the sides and across the feebly lit front of the knoll, apparently concentrating on the bungalow because it housed Emerald's boss and was separate from the rest of the camp. A man, scuttling along beneath the windows, aimed and fired at Ki, but missed. Ki turned, ducking reflexively, just in time to see the man go down.

It had not been Cookie who'd plugged him. Ki, glanc-

177

ing over his shoulder, gave Margot an admiring grin. She was using her late husband's Webley revolver now and was handling it with effectiveness—as Ki could testify.

Suddenly he shouted, "Margot! To your left!"

She stepped back a pace, swiveling, and blasted another man through the chest. She returned Ki's grin with a grateful smile of her own—then three men came at her together through the window just beside her, while a door crashed behind them at the rear.

In a confused and nightmarish tangle of motion, Ki found himself shoved back, fighting, against a wall. There came a cry from Margot; with an erupting fury he stabbed the first man in the throat with the forefinger and middle finger of his left hand, crushing the man's windpipe, crumpling him instantly to the floor. Simultaneously he punched a sideways elbow smash with his right arm, caving in the second man's ribs and stopping his heart. Then he twisted low as Margot blew the head off the third.

Meanwhile, Cookie was resisting the invaders at the rear door, Ki and Margot racing to his aid. They riddled the rear door with bullets, but defiantly one man managed to thrust halfway in, leering as he strove to trigger his pistol. There was a snick of steel, as Cookie snatched up his butcher's cleaver and split open the man's skull. The man reeled backward, the cleaver still buried deep, his gory appearance causing a concerted rout from the stoop.

Now the front door was bursting wide. They hurried to repel the onslaught there, seeing the door nearly wrenched off its hinges by the wedge of burly gunmen all trying to claw in at the same time.

The clash was a brutal mess. Shots cracked, knives snicked, hands grappled for throats. Ki whacked his rifle across an impervious face and almost bent the barrel. The man fell away in a spew of teeth and blood, his countenance mashed worse than Justin Purdue's nose. Margot emptied her revolver, traded it for one a dying gunman had dropped, and emptied it, too. Then she clubbed with it as she searched for a replacement. She accidentally kicked Cookie as he wrestled with a gunman who was as raving mad as he; when next the gunman was glimpsed, his head was missing, for now Ki had drawn his short, curve-bladed *tanto* and was slashing at bellies and limbs with precise strokes.

Kill or be killed!

The Emerald killed voraciously, here in the bungalow and from the buildings below. The raiders, as callous and vicious as they were, still had hopes and promised wages to live for—the camp they were up against had nothing save inflamed desperation. And the odds had evened mightily, the gang having suffered a fierce toll. Dead men lay across doorways, under windows, around the grounds. Empty shells littered everywhere, crunching underfoot. The morning air was overcast with pungent gunsmoke, which was fuming so strongly out of open windows that it appeared as though the interiors were burning.

The raiders began to retreat, drawing away from the buildings and ceasing their attempts to overrun the bungalow. They continued hazing with heavy fire, and Freis' ranting voice was drowning the other shouts as he tried to establish authority, but the damage was done. His gunmen were turning toward their horses at the fringe of the camp, slipping back into habits common to hired killers: If at first you don't succeed, haul ass before it's shot off. And seeing he was being arbitrarily abandoned, Freis swung after them.

"Cover me!" Ki yelled, plunging outside.

Grabbing rifles and reloading, Margot and Cookie began shooting methodically, implacably. And as the jacks became aware of Ki sprinting down the knoll, they joined in protectively, carrying the fight to the gunmen. Yet as Ki sped straight toward Freis, he was an open target for the stymied raiders, and though they were forced to seek shelter and keep low, they sent bullets whistling around him.

Glimpsing Ki as he was mounting, Freis hit saddle and wheeled to face him. A slug scraped hotly across Ki's cheek. He steadied himself just in time to see Freis spur his horse forward, the enraged marshal bending far over, revolver thrust out, firing as he came.

Like a catalyst, it provoked a chain reaction. Gunmen jumped aboard horses, fanning out, while jacks poured from doorways to cut them down. Attackers and defenders became embroiled in open conflict.

Another bullet nipped Ki. He refused to give ground, whipping out one of his daggers instead and flinging it as he ran. Freis' horse thundered past, so close that Ki had to dodge aside. Freis triggered again, and Ki felt the lead clip his shirt sleeve. He twisted, bringing another dagger to bear. Freis yanked his horse about and came charging back, cursing in hard, flat tones. Ki clenched his teeth—gauging distance, speed—and tossed with cool, deliberate aim.

Freis abruptly vanished, toppling backward from the saddle. Someone else rushed down on Ki, firing rapidly. But Freis' riderless horse shied between them, and as the animal swept by, Ki reached up. He gripped the saddlehorn and held on grimly, letting the horse drag him across to a building, one of the bunkhouses, where he let go and rolled up against its wall, crouching a moment to catch his breath.

One swift glance told him the way the fighting was going. Freis was down, but the jacks had recklessly left their cover. The gunmen had the advantage of experience and ruthlessness, and Freis was with them, wounded in the chest but still very much alive.

There was, he thought, only one solution. Gritting his teeth, he straightened and started forward. "Freis!" he called.

Freis heeled to face him, his revolver spitting flame. A slug hissed by Ki's ear; another kicked dust at his feet. He stopped, falling to one knee, and flicked three *shuriken* in swift succession. They landed in a tight pattern; the first slicing deep where Freis' heart should be, the second just above the bridge of his nose, and the third in his larnyx. Freis began to crumple as though deflating and fired his revolver reflexively, blowing a hole in his foot.

Freis' dying caused an effect Ki wanted. One of the gunmen whirled, pistol lifted, but he didn't shoot. He stood there for a split second, gawping, then yelled, "He's down, boys. Our meal ticket's down, and he ain't about to rise. Shit, no!"

That's what Ki wanted. The gunmen milled wildly, those in the saddle turning and starting to ride out, those afoot making a frantic dash for horses. Ki watched, grinning. He knew this kind. They were fighters, but they fought for cash, and with Freis dead, they had no reason to stay.

The gunmen hurtled past Ki, spurring their horses out on the wagon trail, beating a retreat as fast as they could gallop. The frail sunrise spotted them against the forest landscape, but before any of the jacks could take proper aim, the raiders were beyond the field and in the trees, gone from view.

A silence descended—a dry, sucked-out silence.

Slowly Ki stood, scanning the camp and seeing Margot dashing to him. "They're on the run!" she cried, breaking the hush and laughing with shaky relief. "We stood them off, we did!"

"Not without cost," a jack morosely reminded her. As indeed was true. "A damn high price."

"And it looks like we'll hafta pay it again!" Cookie bawled from the bungalow porch. "They're coming back at us."

"Where?"

"The trail! Can't you hear 'em rearing for another run?"

Listening intently, they caught strange scuffling noises echoing faintly from the direction of the wagon trail. Suddenly shots rang out, a splattering of guns as though the raiders were firing up with renewed enthusiasm. Then silence.

"I don't understand this," Margot said grimly. "Why— say, here they come!" She looked about. "This time we'll get kill—"

"Don't! Wait!" Ki knocked a rifle aside before the jack could trigger. "That's Aubrecht out there, and . . . Jessie!"

Peering, they all could now discern the Emerald owner slowly hiking toward them, determinedly supporting and somewhat bent under the weight of Hans Aubrecht. His head lolled and one arm dangled uselessly, but Aubrecht had his other arm wrapped sturdily around Jessie's shoulder, as if it was he who was holding up her. And even at this distance, they could hear him bellowing. "Don't care if you're Queen o' Sheba, Miz Starbuck. If'n you trip again, God help you, when I get well!"

"Alive, the ol' goat's alive," Maxwell shouted happily. "Well, might've knowed. The devil won't have him, an' spit him back."

Behind them followed two other jacks, badly wounded, carried along by Duncan and Rachel. It was apparent now what the recent shots were about. These three jacks were the last survivors of those at the draw and aided by the opportune appearance of Jessie and the Biggses, had confronted the fleeing gunmen while making their painful return to the camp. Later it was learned another jack died in that brief, unexpected skirmish, but so had three more gunmen.

The six had feared they'd find the camp demolished, the defenders annihilated. They let out a cheer as, in response to their plight, the jacks in the camp mounted horses and galloped toward them.

And, some hours after that, when the dead were buried and the wounded were patched and resting, Jessie related the events which led to her and the Biggses' arriving back at camp. She avoided implicating the cartel, however, feeling it to be too complex and disruptive a revelation to disclose now. So she kept silent about the loot Pritt had had and adroitly explained Freis' schemes as though he'd acted as an individual, rather than in cahoots with a criminal conspiracy.

"We reburied the skins and headed straight here, alarmed by Purdue's threat that Freis may well raise a large gang overnight," she said. "It proved all too true, but I think we smashed it. We definitely ended Freis and his shenanigans."

"We also ended McManus' badgering Emerald," Margot remarked. "Since he doesn't legally own his ranch, he'll have to move away."

"Not necessarily. While I was in Grants Pass, I talked with the real owners, the Oregon & California Railroad. They're quite willing to lease Bar M the land, once they cancel the lease with Great Americana for fraud. I'm sure, though, that after this episode, McManus will be much more cooperative." Jessie smiled contentedly. "I'm sure he'll carry on his ranching and we'll carry on our logging like respectable neighbors."

Gerry Shaw flung his cap into the air and gave vent to a reasonable imitation of a cowboy whoop.

Watch for

LONE STAR IN THE CHEROKEE STRIP

forty-fourth novel in the exciting
LONE STAR
series from Jove

coming in April!